S0-CFW-774

"HAVE YOU EVER BEEN GHOST HUNTING BEFORE?"

Bel's laugh was high and musical, just like the rest of her voice. "There aren't any ghosts in Journey's End," she said confidently. "We've had stories, just like every place 'round here. There used to be one about a ghost haunting a lighthouse."

She pointed out to sea, toward the Boundary. "Said she was a girl from the village who did . . . something bad, I don't recall what, and that as punishment, she was set adrift in a boat."

Nolie widened her eyes. "Whoa."

But Bel only shook her head. "It's not real," she said. "We don't even know if the bit about there being a *lighthouse* is real, much less a ghost."

OTHER BOOKS YOU MAY ENJOY

The Apothecary	Maile Meloy
Circus Mirandus	Cassie Beasley
Fish in a Tree	Lynda Mullaly Hunt
The Glass Sentence	S. E. Grove
Matilda	Roald Dahl
Ruby & Olivia	Rachel Hawkins
Savvy	Ingrid Law
A Tangle of Knots	Lisa Graff

JOURNEY'S END

JOURNEY'S END

RACHEL HAWKINS

PUFFIN BOOKS

PUFFIN BOOKS
An imprint of Penguin Random House LLC
375 Hudson Street
New York, New York 10014

First published in the United States of America by G. P. Putnam's Sons,
an imprint of Penguin Random House LLC, 2016
Published by Puffin Books, an imprint of Penguin Random House LLC, 2017

Copyright © 2016 by Rachel Hawkins

Penguin supports copyright. Copyright fuels creativity, encourages diverse voices, promotes
free speech, and creates a vibrant culture. Thank you for buying an authorized edition of this
book and for complying with copyright laws by not reproducing, scanning, or distributing
any part of it in any form without permission. You are supporting writers and allowing
Penguin to continue to publish books for every reader.

THE LIBRARY OF CONGRESS HAS CATALOGED THE G. P. PUTNAM'S SONS EDITION AS FOLLOWS:
Names: Hawkins, Rachel, 1979–, author.
Title: Journey's end / Rachel Hawkins.
Description: New York, NY : G.P. Putnam's Sons, [2016]
Summary: Faced with a mysterious, deadly fog bank in a seaside Scottish
village, new friends Nolie and Bel look for ways to stop it—coming across
an ancient spell that requires magic, a quest, and a sacrifice.
Identifiers: LCCN 2016001030 | ISBN 9780399169601 (hardback)
Subjects: | CYAC: Supernatural—Fiction. | Friendship—Fiction. | Scotland—Fiction. |
BISAC: JUVENILE FICTION / Action & Adventure / General. | JUVENILE FICTION / People
& Places / Europe. | JUVENILE FICTION / Social Issues / Friendship.
Classification: LCC PZ7.H313525 Jo 2016 | DDC [Fic]—dc23
LC record available at https://lccn.loc.gov/2016001030

Puffin Books ISBN 9780147512901

Printed in the United States of America

1 3 5 7 9 10 8 6 4 2

Design by Marikka Tamura

This is a work of fiction. Names, characters, places, and incidents
either are the product of the author's imagination or are used fictitiously,
and any resemblance to actual persons, living or dead, businesses,
companies, events, or locales is entirely coincidental.

For William Moore and William Hawkins,
two guys who love the ocean and spooky stories.

JOURNEY'S END

CHAPTER 1

ALBERT MACLEISH WOKE UP EARLY ON THE MORNING he disappeared.

It had to be early if he was to leave without his mum and da noticing, so it was still murky and dim when he opened the front gate and slipped out into the quiet, rutted lane that ran past his house. It had rained the night before, and he was careful to keep from stepping in the puddles that dotted the road. He'd dressed in the dark that morning, and he'd been in a hurry, slipping on the first pair of shoes he'd found. Unfortunately, those were his good shoes, the ones he wore to church, and Mum would hide him good if he got them dirty.

Moving gingerly, he skipped over one puddle, skirted another. It was barely dawn, but as he passed the other houses on the road, he could see people moving inside them, shadows behind curtains. At the McLeods', his friend Sean's father was already heading down the front steps, fishing pole in hand.

"Morning, Bertie!" he called out, not seeing how Albert winced at the nickname. He'd always been a Bertie, but now that he was nearly thirteen, he'd decided it was high time he was called Albert. Too bad no one in Journey's End seemed to agree.

"Mornin', sir!" he called back. Sean's father was a bigger man than Albert's own da had been, with heavy feet that stomped into the lane, obliterating the little pools of water Albert had been so careful to avoid. As Mr. McLeod clomped closer, one giant foot sent up splatters of rain and mud, dotting Albert's trousers.

He winced again and Mr. McLeod clapped a beefy hand on his shoulder.

"Where you off to so early, lad?"

For a moment, Albert panicked. He hadn't thought to come up with an excuse should anyone see him heading toward the village. The MacLeishes were farmers, not fishermen, so unlike Tom Leslie or James McInnish, he'd have no reason to be down at the docks this time of morning. By all rights, he should be milking Maud or feeding the chickens.

But before he said anything, the front door of the McLeods' swung open, Sean's mum standing there, a bucket dangling from her hand. She looked like Sean, all tiny features and wispy blond hair. "Yer lunch, Robert," she said, the corners of her mouth quirking so that Albert knew this wasn't the first time she'd had to remind Mr. McLeod of something.

Albert used that as an opportunity to hurry on down the lane, and soon the McLeods, their cottage, and any questions they might ask about why a farming boy was walking out to the shore at this time of morning were far behind him.

As the road curved uphill, Albert moved faster, his breath coming out in small white clouds. The air always smelled of salt and sea, but that morning, Albert could also smell the very first beginnings of spring, a rich, loamy green smell that made him smile, and when he crested the hill, he began to whistle a bit.

Journey's End was nestled at the base of the hill, surrounded on its other two sides by rolling green. The sea pressed at its back, crashing against the high, rocky cliffs. There were houses on those cliffs, solid wooden structures that belonged to families much wealthier than Albert's. He'd always liked those houses, how stubbornly they clung to the top of the cliffs, big bay windows jutting out toward the ocean. They made Albert think of tough boys, their chests puffed out as though they were challenging the sea to just *try* to take them down.

Albert's older brother, Edward, had sworn he'd live in one of those houses someday. Edward was gone now, and while Albert liked the big houses on the cliffs, he had no intention of staying in this village when he was older. Sometimes he wondered why anyone did, and if he was the only one who thought there was something a little sad about being born in a place called Journey's End. It seemed like a place where people should end up, not where they started out. He'd tried to ask Edward once, but Edward had just ruffled Albert's hair and told him there were too many thoughts in his head.

He headed down the hill, the road turning from mud and puddles to cobblestones. Over in Wythe, the next village over, they had paved streets. But then, people in Wythe had automobiles, too, and no one in Journey's End—not even the people in the houses on the cliffs—could afford an automobile.

The sun was higher when Albert reached the village proper, and he could see Mrs. Collins opening the door to her shop. She waved at Albert as he passed, but thankfully didn't ask what he was about.

The docks were to his right, and Albert skirted those, turning instead to the left and the little trail that wound down to the beach. There wasn't much shoreline in Journey's End, and what existed was covered in sharp pebbles that Albert could feel even through his nice shoes.

He stood there, hands in his pockets, looking out at the water. A mile offshore, a wall of gray rose up from the water. It covered the sea below, climbing high enough to mingle with the clouds, and no one could have mistaken it for a regular fog bank. It was too solid, for one thing, never drifting or dissipating like fog usually did. The sun never burned off this wall of mist, which seemed as permanent as the rocks on the shore, as the cliffs that stretched over the sea.

But more than that, there was the feeling you got when you looked at what everyone in Journey's End was trying so hard not to talk about. Not that anyone could avoid talking about the fog for long, of course, but when they did, it was said in a whisper—*the fog*—that slid through people lips, then hung heavy in the air. Even now, Albert felt the hairs on the back of his neck stand up, and there was a sick kind of swirling in his stomach, the same he'd felt the day Edward had dared him to jump from the hayloft. He'd done it, but the twinge in his ankle reminded him what a foolish decision it had been.

He hoped this decision wasn't that stupid. Or painful.

For as long as Albert had been alive, the fog had clung to the rocky island where the lighthouse stood, like the island was a master keeping its beast—the fog—on a tight leash.

But sometime during the winter, the light had gone out. They hadn't been able to see it at first—the fog was too thick for that—but slowly, the gray had begun creeping closer, sliding across the waters of the Caillte Sea . . . slowly, but surely.

All his life, Albert had heard the legend of the light-house, that its light was what kept the fog at bay, but he'd never truly believed that. He wasn't sure anyone did. But as the fog slithered closer, so too did the story of its light, something to do with a witch and an ancient curse.

There was something else, too, something that Albert didn't really understand. When the fog had started its creep toward the land, some of the people in the village went to a meeting in the town hall—a meeting that was meant to be secret.

Edward had still been here then, and he and Albert had sneaked down to the hall, trying to watch through the cracks in the slats, but all they'd seen were some of the men from the village standing up, a tall, dark-haired girl in their midst, her face pale, her clothes odd.

"Did you put it out yourself?" Albert had heard a voice ask. He'd thought it was Mr. MacMillan, the man who owned the dry goods store in town, but he hadn't been able to see. "Is that why ye've come back?"

That was the part that had seemed so odd to Albert. Come back? From where? He was sure he'd never seen the girl before in his life, and near every face in Journey's End was known to him.

Their da had caught him and Edward then, and the hiding they'd both gotten had nearly driven the memory of the mysterious meeting from their minds.

Then Edward's friend Davey McKissick had taken a boat out to light the light himself.

Davey hadn't come back. Neither had Davey's father when he went looking for him.

And then Edward had declared that he'd light the light. The fog had seemed more dangerous by then, creeping close to shore, and more stories were told now, in louder voices. Stories about the fog sliding through the village, making ships and houses disappear. Warnings that if it came into the village, it would snatch people from their very beds.

More tales Albert had never really believed in, but looking out now, he could feel it, pressing in with curling fingers.

The waves were gentler here in the sheltered cove, but they still sent bursts of salt spray into the air as they crashed against the smaller boulders near the shore. Albert was a farm boy in his heart, and looking out at that gray water, he longed for mud underneath his shoes, for the sweet smell of hay in his nose.

But he knew this was the best chance he would have, and if he didn't start now, he would lose his nerve altogether.

Bending down, he removed his shoes, then his socks, setting both on a high, flat rock nearby, hoping that would keep them safe from the worst of the spray. Later, the group of men sent to look for Albert—Sean's da among them—would find his shoes. They would be all of him anyone would ever find, and his mum would keep them on the mantelpiece until the cold day in December 1928 when her broken heart finally stopped beating.

He hopped down the beach much the same way he'd hopped down the path to the sea, skirting rocks instead of pebbles, but his feet got scraped up anyway, the salt water making every step sting.

Over the years, the sea had carved hollows into the cliff side. Edward had said some of these caves went back for miles, turning into tunnels that ran underneath Journey's End, and that if you weren't careful, you could get lost forever underground. Albert hated those stories, and as he passed one of the bigger hollows in the rock, he shivered.

The cave Albert was looking for wasn't very deep at all. It went back only a few feet, but he still swallowed hard as he ducked inside the dark opening. Here, the sound of the sea was both louder and more distant, like putting his ear against a seashell, and Albert worked quickly, wanting to be out of the cave as quickly as possible.

The little rowboat hidden behind a shelf of rock had seen better days, and its hull (once painted blue, he thought) was now a faded and scratched gray. A handful of barnacles clung to the side, and the entire vessel smelled strongly of rotting fish, but Albert smiled as he tugged the boat out of its hiding place and toward the sea.

He had found it just a few days ago, not long after Edward had vanished into the fog. Even though the Bible said stealing was wrong, and Albert's mum and da would both have taken the strap to him, he told himself that it wasn't stealing. It was *finding*. Albert had kept his eyes peeled in the village for any signs announcing the loss of a rowboat, but there hadn't been any, and Albert had started to think of the little boat as his. The *Selkie*, it was called, the words painted in curling black script.

As he dragged the *Selkie* to the shallows, Albert's heart thudded in his chest and he tried very hard not to think that maybe the reason no one had reported it missing was because whomever it had belonged to was dead, lost out there beyond the fog bank.

The frigid water was lapping against Albert's ankles now, the boat thudding against his shins as he tried to steady it with one hand. The oars rested in the bottom of the boat, and they rattled as Albert climbed inside.

For a moment, he sat there on the splintered seat, the boat rocking but not yet being tugged out into the ocean. His breath was coming fast now, and not from dragging the boat. It was fear. But nestled right up next to that fear,

9

as tight as the barnacles on the side of his stolen—*found*—boat, was hope. This would work.

It had to.

Albert lifted his eyes once more to the rolling bank of gray blotting out the horizon. Out there in the fog was a high, rocky crag. He couldn't see it now—the fog was too thick—but atop that crag was the lighthouse. Someone had lit it once, saving Journey's End, and Albert knew this was the only way. It had taken Davey McKissick and his da. It had taken Edward. But it would *not* take Albert. He wouldn't let it. Hadn't he found this boat just after Edward vanished? Wasn't that some kind of sign that he was meant to take it, and go after his brother?

He hoisted the oars, pushing off one of the nearby boulders. Behind him, Journey's End, the village he'd known all his life, the village that would one day put his picture on a wall with all the other sons and daughters, brothers and sisters, it had lost to the sea, receded into the fog.

And Albert rowed off and became a mystery.

FROM "THE SAD TALE OF CAIT McINNISH,"
CHAPTER 13,
Legends of the North

CAIT HAD NEVER BELIEVED IN THE FAIRY STORIES.

If she had, neither she nor the boy might have died, but Cait was a sensible girl, and when she saw the old woman washing the boy's clothes in the stream, she had thought nothing of it. She and Rabbie were making their way back from the village, his hand small and warm in hers, and as they'd passed, Cait had simply thought the washerwoman must have had a grandson of her own, another bonny boy with a blue tunic marked with the stag of the laird's house.

Had she known her stories, she would've recognized the washerwoman as a Bean-Nighe, the fairy who came as an omen of death, washing the clothes of the doomed in streams and rivers, and it might have made her eyes sharper, her feet swifter.

Maybe later in the day, when they'd come back to the castle, she would've been fast enough to catch Rabbie when he ran past her, giggling, the sun shining on his copper-bright hair. Maybe her fingers would've caught his tunic (*blue, so blue, blue as his eyes, blue as the sky he was rushing to meet*). Maybe she would've caught him before he stumbled, arms spinning as he pitched toward the castle's open window.

Maybe, maybe, maybe.

Cait thought the word enough that it sounded like a spell itself, a constant chant in her mind.

But she did not catch him, and even though that morning she had not recognized the Bean-Nighe for what it was, the fairy's warning came true all the same.

If this were one of those fairy stories Cait did not believe, the boy might've sprouted wings that would have saved him at the last moment, when he'd gone soaring over the rocky cliff and icy sea. He would be revealed as a changeling, a fairy himself, blessed. Protected.

This is not one of those stories.

CHAPTER 2

"SO YOU'RE SURE PEOPLE LIVE HERE?" NOLEN STANHOPE asked her father as they drove down the bumpy road leading to Journey's End. A few houses dotted the landscape, but they were hardly more than blurry shapes in the fog, and Nolie leaned closer to the window, her breath making its own fog. "On purpose?"

The car hit another pothole, and Nolie jounced in her seat, running her finger through the little cloud she'd made on the glass.

"Yup," her father told her, pushing his glasses up his nose with one finger. "Few hundred of 'em."

Nolie knew that, of course. When she'd heard she'd be spending the summer with her dad, out here literally at the *end of the world*, she'd done her reading. What she'd learned had made her a little less excited for this trip: there were 453 people currently living in the village of Journey's End, it rained roughly 300 days of the year, and even in the height of summer, temperatures rarely rose above sixty degrees Fahrenheit.

At home in Georgia, the summers were hot and sweaty and smelled like chlorine and freshly cut grass.

In Scotland, the salty scent of the sea snuck in despite the rolled-up windows, and underneath that, another, bitter smell. Almost like smoke.

Nolie liked it.

And she liked the idea of being here in Scotland for the summer. Back home, she'd be spending June through August trying not to die of heatstroke and talking her mom out of sending her back to those weird little day camps at the community center. Learning how to make decoupage boxes had been fun when she was ten or eleven, but now that she was twelve? International travel seemed like a *much* better way to spend the summer.

Tearing off the sticker that announced she was an Unaccompanied Minor, she turned back to the book in her lap, a collection of ghost stories her dad had brought her when she'd met him at the airport in Inverness. "I remembered you liked spooky things," he'd told her, and she'd grinned. Nolie didn't just like spooky things; she *loved* them. Her favorite TV shows all involved people with night-vision cameras and EVP recorders in scary old houses, and she'd actually loaded five episodes of *Chasing Spirits* on her phone before leaving for Scotland.

Her dad, being a scientist, had never been all that crazy about ghosts or monsters, so she thought the book might be a kind of peace offering, a "hey, sorry I haven't seen you in six months because I was in Scotland studying fog" present.

He'd also brought her a stuffed animal, a sheep wearing a little blue T-shirt that read *Stand baaaaack!*

Apparently that was supposed to be some sort of joke about "the Boundary," the big fog bank off the coast that her dad had come here to study. She'd read a lot about that, too, wanting to know just what it was about this place her dad found so fascinating. She'd only had to look at a couple of websites before she totally got it. The Boundary was like the Bermuda Triangle, a place where people went missing with no real explanation. And it had just showed up a few hundred years ago, out of nowhere, upping the whole Super Creepy and Mysterious thing a lot.

Still, selling sheep with T-shirts joking about it seemed a little weird. Maybe that was what people thought was funny out here in . . . could you even call a place like this "the boonies"? She would have said that at home, but it usually referred to a place in the country where everyone lived in trailers and had cows. This place seemed even farther away than that, and Nolie wasn't sure there was a word for what Journey's End was.

Nolie turned to her dad. "Mom said the house is on the beach?" She'd been looking forward to that. The water would be too cold for swimming, but she could still wrap up in a sweatshirt and watch the ocean.

Her dad nodded. "It is, yeah. But the fog is so thick that you wouldn't even know the Caillte Sea was there if you couldn't hear it."

Nolie had known the name of the sea from the books she'd read, but she'd been pronouncing it "KALE-teh." In her dad's mouth, the word came out more like "*Kyle*-che," and Nolie sighed. She hadn't realized coming here would involve learning a whole new language, too.

"Caillte," she repeated, trying to get it right, and her dad smiled, showing off his slightly crooked front teeth. Like Nolie, his eyes were blue and there was a smattering of freckles across his cheeks. Underneath his cap (this totally embarrassing plaid thing that made him look like an old-fashioned newspaper boy), his hair was a lighter shade of Nolie's own bright red.

His eyebrows were red, too, and he waggled them over his glasses at Nolie now. "Good job, kiddo. We'll have you talking like a local before you know it."

Her dad turned left onto something he called the "high street," but it was actually pretty low, the road curving down into a valley, and green hills rising up on both sides, cutting off Nolie's view of the ocean.

As her dad stopped the [...]
bright yellow shopping bag [...]
ticed a man standing on the [...]
over his chest as he looked a[...]
really. The man's face was red[...]
eyes, but Nolie didn't miss t[...]
giving them.

And when she looked back [...]
lady passing in front of them w[...]

Nolie's dad sighed.

"Just a heads-up, kiddo," he said. "I'm not exactly the most popular guy in Journey's End at the moment." The car was lurching forward now that the way was clear.

"It's not a big deal," he went on to say, drumming his fingers on the steering wheel. "Just that things between the Institute and the town have always been a little tense, and lately, they've been *really* tense. We've been trying some new experiments, testing out new equipment, and no one in town is really a fan of that."

"Why not?" Nolie asked.

Her dad shook his head. "Lots of reasons, I think. Main one being that if we actually figure out what's causing the fog, it might make it seem a little less mysterious, and that could affect tourism. That's how most of the people in town make their money, chartering boats out to see it, selling stuff like that." He nodded at the book and the if you see me getting ugly looks,

 was about your hat," Nolie joked, and her
 over at her, smiling.

 have you in one of these hats before the summer is
ut, just you wait," he promised, and Nolie grinned back.

The car was moving uphill now, and once again, the
Caillte Sea spread out below them, gray and rocky.

"What does it mean?" Nolie asked. "*Caillte?*" The car
drove slowly past a lot of gray brick buildings with big
front windows that all displayed a *lot* of plaid, and in one,
some cheap plastic beach toys, too. Where was Ye Olde
Walmart? Nolie wondered. Surely people in Journey's
End needed *stuff*.

"It means 'lost,'" Dad replied, just as the car passed a
place called Gifts from the End of the World. Judging
from the display in the window, that was where Nolie's
stuffed sheep had come from, and she twisted in her seat,
trying to get a better look into the shop. But then they
were turning again, following a narrow road out of the
main village and up toward the cliffs.

"That's kind of creepy." The car hit another pothole,
and Nolie nearly bit her tongue. "*The Lost Sea*." It made her
shiver to say it, but in the good way. Definitely the kind
of place where an episode of *Chasing Spirits* could happen.
Did they sell night-vision cameras around here?

Nodding, her dad turned down another lane, this one covered in gravel that rattled underneath the tires. "The name is creepy, but fitting. Lots of people *have* gotten lost out there."

Nolie thought about mentioning that people went missing in every ocean ever, but she was afraid that would sound mean, so she just made an agreeing noise and propped her heels on the edge of her seat.

They rattled and bumped down the lane, twisting and turning, until her dad pulled up in front of a big white house with navy shutters and a wraparound front porch. It was narrow, but tall, and looked a lot older than the house Nolie shared with her mom back in Georgia.

Her dad must have read her thoughts, because as they got out of the car, he smiled and said, "Built in 1854. Which actually makes it one of the newer houses in Journey's End." He gestured farther down the cliff, and Nolie saw several other houses that looked almost identical to this one. "The Institute bought all of them when they set up the research center here. Uses them as homes for those of us who work out here full-time." He pointed to another house, far enough away that it was only a white dot against the bright green of the hills. The house was situated on a little rise and closer to the cliffs than the others. "That's it right there," he told her. "The Institute."

"It's just another house," Nolie said, and her dad gave an easy shrug.

"We've never been able to get a permit to build a new building, so we use what we can. It's the second-biggest house in Journey's End."

Turning, Nolie pushed her hair back from where it was blowing in her face. "What's the biggest one?"

Dad smiled and folded his arms on top of the car. "Old manor house on the outskirts of town. You'd like it."

Nolie made a mental note to see it when she got a chance.

For now, she walked past the car and skirted the house altogether, walking around the side where she could get a view of the ocean and the massive, rolling fog bank a few miles out.

"That's it, huh?"

At first glance, the Boundary just looked like fog. Lots of it, sure, blotting out the horizon, rising to the sky, stretching so far that Nolie couldn't see past it on either side, but the longer she stared at it, the stranger it seemed. It was thicker than any fog she'd ever seen, and it seemed to roll and churn without actually moving forward.

Her dad clapped a hand on her shoulder, and Nolie leaned toward him a bit. It was nice, finally being with her dad after six months of not seeing him, and until this second, she hadn't realized how much she'd missed him.

"That's it," he confirmed, and when she looked up at him, he was grinning dreamily out at the sea, like he was looking at a puppy or a pretty girl or anything but a giant cloud of fog that maybe ate people.

"It doesn't look so scary," Nolie lied.

Dad laughed. "It's not supposed to be scary. Not anymore, at least. It's fascinating and mysterious, but not scary."

Nolie wasn't sure how fascinating it was, but it was definitely mysterious. A giant ball of fog that had hovered there off the shore since who knew when, apparently. A big mass of cloud that, if you sailed into it, wouldn't let you sail back out. There was even a no-fly zone established over it since a few planes had gone missing back in the seventies. But then, for the most part, no one ever had a reason to fly over this tiny spit of land. Not for the first time, Nolie wondered why this big wall of mist was so much more interesting to her dad than anything in Georgia.

More interesting than Nolie and her mom.

"I could take you over to the Institute later," Dad offered. "Show you a little bit of what I do out here."

Nolie had taken three separate flights just to get to Scotland, and then there'd been the three-hour drive to Journey's End. She was tired and weirded out, and had a little bit of a day-after-Christmas feeling going on.

"I think I want to just hang out for now," she said, shaking her head.

The frown that crossed her dad's face was only there for a second, but Nolie saw it, and it made her feel guilty.

"Can I walk down to the beach?" she asked, hoping that might make him happy. That way, she could still be alone, but she wouldn't be sulking in her room, or making him think she was disappointed. She'd be *exploring*.

Nolie could see her dad thinking about it, and she moved a little closer. "I promise not to get in the water."

That made Dad smile a little. "Oh, I'm not worried about that. You dip one toe in, you'd run out screaming. It almost never goes above about fifteen degrees, even in the summer."

"*Fifteen?*" Nolie asked, looking back out at the water, trying to imagine how it could be that cold in the summer.

"Oh, sorry," her dad said, shaking his head. "Fifteen degrees Celsius. That's about sixty degrees to you." Nolie wrinkled her nose at that. Sixty degrees was better than fifteen, but still. What was the point of a beach if you couldn't swim in the ocean? Mom always took her to Tybee Island in the summer, where the ocean felt like a bath, and the sun made freckles pop out on her shoulders and the bridge of her nose.

But after all those hours on planes, Nolie could use some quiet time to stretch her legs.

Even if it was on a frozen beach with man-eating fog.

But before Dad could give her a yes or no, the phone attached to his belt rang. He held up one finger, answering it while Nolie looked back at the sea.

She wondered just how many people had been lost. Her dad had said there was a memorial in town, and they kept records at the Institute. She definitely wanted to check that out.

A movement down on the shore caught her eye, and Nolie leaned a little closer. Looked like she wasn't the only one who'd thought about taking a walk today. A boy was wandering along the water's edge. It was foggy down there, but not too bad, and she could see his dark hair, make out the puzzled expression on his face when he glanced up toward the cliffs. He was dressed awfully well for beach strolling, in Nolie's opinion, and she wondered if that was another thing she needed to learn about Journey's End. Did everyone go to the beach in their Sunday best?

Turning back to her dad, Nolie decided she didn't want to walk on the beach after all. But it apparently didn't matter, since he was already moving back to the car, waving for her to follow him. "The Institute," he said by way of explanation. "Need to get back for a little bit."

"Why?"

Her dad wiggled the cell phone at her. "Not sure,

really. Connection cut out before Burkhart could tell me what was going on. That's the problem with Journey's End; phones never work quite right. Same for TV and the internet."

"Right," Nolie said. "Mom mentioned that. She even bought me a stationery set so I could write letters." Mom had actually promised to send a letter as soon as Nolie left, so she was hoping to get one soon. As nice as it was to be spending time with Dad again, she already missed her mom.

Dad raised his eyebrows. "That'll be fun, then. Very old-school. We *do* get fairly decent internet at the Institute, so if you wanna email your friends or . . . or Facebook or—"

"I'm twelve, Dad. Mom lets me stay at our house by myself all the time."

But Dad just gave an easy shrug. "That's your mom," he said. "Go ahead and get in. We won't stay too long."

"I'm tired, Dad," she argued. "And, I mean, no offense, but I don't feel like hanging out in your office today."

She expected a fight, but instead, Dad walked around and opened her car door—the wrong side; she wasn't sure if she'd ever get used to that—and said, "Make you a deal: I'll drop you in the city center. You can look around, and I won't be gone long."

Nolie thought about mentioning that she'd probably be safer in his house than wandering a strange village on her own, but looking around did sound better than going to work with her dad. She slid back into the car seat and closed her door, her book of ghost stories and stuffed sheep tumbling to the floorboard.

"I'll bring you up to work tomorrow," Dad offered, "after you've had a chance to get your feet back under you."

As they drove down the hill, she turned to look over her shoulder. From this angle, she couldn't see the water, and she thought again of that boy on the beach. She could have sworn he'd been wearing suspenders. Was that a Scottish thing?

The water out of sight, the only thing Nolie could see now was the fog—the Boundary—up beyond the green hill.

CHAPTER 3

BEL KNEW IT WAS WEIRD TO HAVE A FAVORITE DEAD person, but since she spent every afternoon looking at pictures of dead people, it was bound to happen.

She moved her dust cloth over the boy's photograph, making sure the glass was extra shiny. The little plaque under his frame declared that his name was Albert Mac-Leish, but Bel knew everyone had called him Al. He'd died in 1918, and there was no one from his family left in Journey's End, but Bel had spent most of her life looking at his face on the back wall of her parents' souvenir shop, so she felt pretty confident that he was an Al. There was something about his eyes and the way he was smiling without seeming to smile that struck Bel as . . . Al-ish.

"There you go, Al," she said out loud, giving his frame one more polish. "Spic-and-span."

Moving on to the next photograph, Bel sighed. If Al was her favorite dead person, Edna Herbert, 1860–1918, was her least. She didn't like the old woman's scowl or how tight her bun was.

So Edna didn't get much of a shine, but Davey McKissick (1898–1918) did, especially since he had been Bel's great-grandfather's uncle. Bel was also careful to give Al's brother, Edward (1900–1918), some extra attention. All in all, there were six photo portraits at the back of the shop, reminders of an awful year when the Boundary had been more troublesome than ever before. Of course, a lot more than six people had died in the choppy waters of the Caillte Sea over the years, but these were the people the village still remembered, and Bel liked that when her grandad opened this shop, he'd decided to make a wee memorial for them.

Of course, it was a bit tacky that the memorial was the back wall of Gifts from the End of the World, and those somber faces were crammed in with shelves of snow globes and stuffed sheep wearing T-shirts, but no one had ever suggested moving the pictures elsewhere.

Bel's mum said it was because the village wanted all those tourists to remember that this was a dangerous place. A sad place, sometimes. But when Bel watched people's eyes skate over the wall of photos as they dug through a display of silly socks, she wasn't sure the memorial was serving its purpose.

Still, she liked the days when Mum sent her to dust the pictures, because it was a quiet, easy job. Now that she was twelve, Mum said she could run the cash register this summer, and Bel was already dreading it. Working with money always made her nervous, especially when there were lines of people. No, give Bel her duster and the row of photographs, and she was a lot happier.

She was also glad that the shop gave her a good excuse for not having that much free time this summer, but that thought just made her sad, so she pushed it away, focusing again on those photographs.

The little bell over the door rang, and Bel turned to see her older brother Jaime walking in. He had the collar of his coat turned up, his sandy-blond hair—the same color as Bel's—mussed from the wind.

"Brutal out there already," he said, ducking behind the counter. He came back with his gloves clutched in one hand, waving them at her. "Thought I could get away without wearing them, but it's *cold*, and Dad says it's a good ten degrees colder offshore."

While Bel and her younger brother, Jack, helped their mum in the gift shop, Jaime worked with their dad on the tour boat. The McKissicks had lived in Journey's End for nearly five hundred years, and they'd all been fishermen until Bel's grandad came up with the idea of turning their fishing boat into a charter that could take tourists out to the Boundary.

Bel looked toward the huge window that took up almost the entire front wall of Gifts from the End of the World. It was gray and damp outside, the wind blowing harder than usual.

"You and Dad are taking the boat out?" she asked Jaime, walking to the shelf just behind the counter and flicking on another lamp. Mum didn't believe in overhead lighting ("Makes everything look cheap," she always said), so the store was dotted with lamps in all shapes and sizes. The one behind Bel featured a wide-eyed china shepherdess topped with a pale pink shade, its light a rosy spill against the shelves of souvenir teapots.

"Yeah," Jaime answered, a grin splitting his face. Like their dad and oldest brother, Simon, Jaime loved the sea, and didn't seem to mind how much time he spent ferrying visitors back and forth from the harbor to the Boundary.

As he walked past Bel, he ruffled her hair, an annoying habit he'd started once he'd turned sixteen and Simon had left for university. He clearly considered it big-brothery, but Bel just shoved his hand away with a roll of her eyes.

"Where's Mum?" he asked, and Bel jerked her head toward the door, indicating the café just across the way.

"Lunch with Mrs. Frey. She'll be back in a few if you want to talk to her."

Jaime shook his head. "Nah. Just wondering." He turned his grin back to her. "So you're in charge this afternoon, eh?"

"For the next half an hour, anyway."

"Fair enough," he replied, before glancing back at the door. "Only got a few on the boat today, so you won't have many folk coming in to buy all of our cheap plastic crap."

With a gasp, Bel leaned, covering the ears of one of the stuffed sheep lining the counter, all of them wearing T-shirts that read *Stand baaaaack!*

"Jaime! How dare you call Lambert and his brethren *crap?* You'll hurt his wee fluffy feelings."

Her brother laughed at that. Then the bell over the door was ringing again as he opened it, and he was gone.

Watching him, Bel's smile slipped just a bit. The weather was so gross today, and she didn't like the idea of both him and her dad out to sea. Who wanted to be out on a boat on a day like today? But Bel had long ago stopped trying to figure out the people who vacationed in Journey's End. She loved it here, but it was her home. Coming all this way to see a fog bank seemed mental.

Still, as Bel picked up her duster and went back to the pictures, she shot another glance at Albert MacLeish. "Keep everybody safe out there today, okay, Al?"

It was a good thing she was alone in the store; Bel's mum never would've stood for Bel asking pictures of dead people for help. Like everyone born in Journey's End, Fiona McKissick was practical, with little patience for superstition. Sometimes Bel wondered if growing up so close to something that actually *felt* magical and mysterious made them that way. Like if they gave in to just a little bit of eccentricity, next thing you knew, there'd be a maypole in the city center and they'd be sacrificing sheep to the full moon or something.

As she moved away from the back wall, Bel could hear voices outside, girls talking and laughing. She looked out the window, and a group of three girls walking down the sidewalk were close enough that Bel could make them out.

There was Cara McLendon, Alice Beattie, and, walking just a bit ahead, her dark hair standing out against the gray, Leslie Douglas. Until just a few months ago, Leslie had been Bel's best friend, but in March, something had changed, something Bel still couldn't explain. All she knew was that one day, she had walked to school with Leslie like she'd been doing since they were six, and the next, Leslie had left early and walked with Alice instead.

Alice had been new in Journey's End, her parents having moved from Wythe to open an arcade for the tourists. Bel knew Leslie had liked the other girl immediately, but it was still a surprise to see how much they were hanging out. Even weirder when Cara McLendon started walking with them, too. Bel and Leslie had known Cara since nursery school, but they'd never hung out with her before.

And then at lunch, Leslie had started sitting with the other two girls, choosing a table with just three chairs so that even if Bel *had* wanted to sit with them, she would've had to drag a chair over, something too embarrassing to even think about.

They hadn't talked about it, and there hadn't been a fight or an argument. Just a sort of vanishing act that made Bel feel like all her insides were on the outside.

And then the girls stopped outside the shop, and her insides weren't just on the outside, they were all twisted up.

Please don't come in, please don't come in, she chanted to herself, but apparently luck wasn't on Bel's side today.

The bell chimed, and Alice, Cara, and Leslie came piling into the store, Leslie just a little bit behind the other two.

"Do you sell brollies in here?" Alice asked, not even bothering to say hi. Bel watched the way the other girls' eyes skimmed over the stuff in the store quickly. Suddenly all the little knickknacks that Bel had always thought looked cute felt like exactly what Jaime had called them—cheap plastic crap.

"We have a few?" Bel offered, then took a deep breath, stepping forward. This was her shop, and she wasn't going to let Alice make her feel bad here.

"We do," she said more firmly, gesturing toward the tall metal can of umbrellas to Alice's left, just next to three racks of postcards.

"I told you they did," Leslie muttered to Alice, and Bel glanced over at her.

"Remember that day we opened them all and made a wee fort?" Bel asked, almost without thinking.

Leslie's pale, round cheeks flushed red, and her eyes darted to Alice. "We were, like, seven," she said, and Bel knew she was explaining herself to Alice, not talking to Bel.

They hadn't been seven. It had been last summer, and it had been fun, the two of them building a sort of tent out of brollies behind the counter, giggling.

But seeing the way Alice's upper lip curled slightly, Bel suddenly wished she hadn't even mentioned it.

"Are they all plaid?" Alice asked, sweeping a hand over the handles of the umbrellas, making them rattle in the can.

"Yeah," Bel said, knowing that if she offered up the

green ones with handles that looked like the Loch Ness monster, the girls would act even more disgusted.

"Never mind, then," Alice said. "Honestly, I'd rather just get wet."

She turned toward the door, and Bel willed herself not to frown or, worse, give in to the lip wobble she could feel coming. Instead, she shrugged and leaned against the counter. "Suit yerself, then," she said, and Leslie shot her another look before the three of them were back out onto the damp, windy street.

Sighing, Bel turned her back on the door, looking at the pictures of the missing again. "Did any of you ever have these problems?" she asked their solemn faces, then shook her head at herself. She was being silly, talking to the pictures. Just as silly as she'd been to make an umbrella fort, probably.

The bell over the door rang again, and Bel whirled around, afraid Leslie and her new friends had come back. What if they'd overhead her talking to the pictures? But when she looked over, there was an unfamiliar girl standing in the doorway.

She was obviously a tourist. Bel knew pretty much all the kids in Journey's End, but it wasn't just the girl's unfamiliar face that told Bel she was new in town. It was her wellies.

Everyone in Journey's End owned a pair of Wellington boots—between the rain and mud, the sea and the sand, they were a necessity—but they were usually black or gray. Bel's own were a dull shade of green closer to brown.

This girl was decked out in bright purple wellies printed with big yellow daisies, and they gleamed in the lamplight, squeaking a little as the girl walked forward. She looked to be about Bel's age, and her red hair was pulled back in a ponytail. As Bel watched, the girl wandered over to the display of stuffed sheep, her lips lifting in a little smile.

"Hiya," Bel called out, and the girl jumped.

"Oh. Um, hi."

Even though her hair was back, the girl went to tuck it behind her ear, her fingers skating over thin air.

Bel laid her duster down, wiping her hands on the seat of her jeans. "Can I help you with something?"

The girl continued to glance around the shop, her eyes wide, and Bel smiled. "I know, it's a lot of stuff."

Nodding slowly, the girl turned in a little half circle. "For sure. I was, uh, actually looking for books?"

She was American, Bel noted with some surprise. They didn't get that many American tourists, although some of the scientists at the Institute came from the States.

"What kind of books?" Bel asked, and the girl thrust her hands into the pockets of her gray jacket.

"Ghost story stuff," she said, and then walked to the metal rack of paperbacks set up near the door. "I have this one." She tapped the cover of *Ghosts of the Boundary.* "But really, anything you've got would be good."

If there was one thing the shop definitely had, it was creepy books, and Bel went around quickly, gathering them up. *Mysteries and Legends, Journey's End: The Village at the End of the World, Monsters of the Minch.*

When she handed them over, the redheaded girl's eyes went wide. "Oh, wow," she said. "This is *awesome.*"

Bel didn't think there was much awesome in those books, but she liked seeing a fellow book lover. Chewing her lip, Bel thought for a second before grinning and saying, "If you want something to read that's *not* about ghosts, I have something."

She dashed behind the counter and reached down, riffling through the stacks of paper bags and those boxes of bookmarks that had never sold very well, until she found what she was looking for.

The paperback was slightly tattered, and the cover had been mended with tape in one corner, but the girl didn't seem to notice as she took the book, her eyes lighting up.

"This looks good," the girl said, turning it over to look at the back. "*Starcatcher Academy,*" she read aloud.

"It's my favorite," Bel told her, bouncing on the balls of her feet a bit. "Aliens pick these human kids to go to a special school on their planet so they can, like, train them as spaceship captains and stuff. It's *ace*. And that's just the first one in the series; there's ten of them altogether."

The girl smiled back. "I could use some aliens with my ghosts. Thanks." She glanced back over her shoulder toward the window and the drizzle outside.

"Is it always like this?"

Bel nodded, her hair brushing her jaw. "Yeah. Rains at least once a day here, usually more." Then she leaned a little closer. "Although it seems particularly nasty today." Once again, her thoughts turned to Jaime and her dad, out on the boat.

"Are you on vacation here?" she asked the girl, wondering if maybe her parents were also headed out toward the Boundary this afternoon.

But the girl shook her head. "Not exactly. My dad is a scientist? At the Institute?"

That was a surprise. The Institute had dominated life in Journey's End ever since Bel was born, but she had never met anyone who worked there, nor anyone who knew people who did. The scientists, who lived in the big houses on the cliffs, tended to stay to themselves. They did their shopping in Wythe rather than the village, although Mum had mentioned that she thought one of the scientists had come in the other day to buy a stuffed sheep.

Bel remembered the way the girl had smiled at the sheep, and wondered if maybe that had been her dad.

"Oh, aye," Bel said now, folding her arms across her chest. "The Institute. I've never been up there."

The girl looked at the door again. "Me neither. I'm Nolie, by the way."

"Nolie," Bel repeated, though the name sounded a lot different when she said it. "I'm Bel."

"That's a great name," Nolie replied, and Bel shrugged, self-conscious.

Nolie was still smiling when her eyes slid past Bel's face and to the back wall of the shop. "Whoa," she said, her voice dropping. "What is . . . what's that?"

Rubbing the back of her neck, Bel shrugged. "Just the memorial wall. People we lost in the village before the Institute came."

A crease formed between Nolie's brows. "Okay, but that kid isn't dead."

She gestured with the book, and Bel realized she was pointing at Albert.

Bel widened her eyes and walked over to the wall, tapping Albert's frame gently. "Albert MacLeish?"

When Nolie nodded, Bel looked back at the photograph. "No, he's proper dead. See?" She ran her finger over the gold plate at the bottom. "1918. He went out fishing or something and never came back."

Nolie moved closer, squinting at the picture. "I saw him on the beach," she said confidently. "Today."

CHAPTER 4

IT HAD ALREADY BEEN A GROSS GRAY DAY WHEN NOLIE'S dad had dropped her off at the store, but as she waited on the sidewalk while Bel switched the sign on the door to CLOSED, a sort of thin drizzle started up, coating her hair and clothes with a fine mist.

It was an eerie feeling, like being inside a cloud, and Nolie huddled a little deeper inside her jacket, a grin already making her cheeks ache.

Mist and now a *ghost*. Scotland was totally turning out to be awesome.

"I promise it won't take long," she told Bel, "and it'll be good to have you there as, like, an expert witness and stuff."

The sign situated, Bel turned around, shoving her hands into her pockets.

"'Expert witness'?" she echoed, and Nolie made what she hoped was a very serious face as she gave her a solemn nod.

"The person most familiar with the dead boy," she intoned, and one corner of Bel's mouth lifted, like she was trying not to smile.

"I don't know about that," she said, "but all right, let's go."

Nolie liked the way the word "right" sounded coming from Bel. She rolled the R, making the word sound almost like singing.

Despite the rain, Bel marched confidently down the sidewalk, swerving around trash cans and signs advertising boat trips and guided tours of the caves lining the shores of Journey's End, and Nolie followed in her footsteps.

"How long have you lived here?" Nolie asked, and Bel turned to glance over her shoulder.

"My whole life. There have been McKissicks in Journey's End for hundreds of years."

"Oh," Nolie replied, unsure of what else to say to that.

"What about you?" Bel asked just as they reached the fountain in the center of the square. It appeared to be some kind of sea monster, spitting water up into the misty sky.

"I'm from Georgia," she told Bel as they skirted the fountain, and Bel veered right, heading off the sidewalk and onto a path of sand and gravel. "But *my* family hasn't been there for hundreds of years or anything."

Bel slowed down, letting Nolie catch up; as soon as Nolie came up beside her, Bel reached out and pressed a hand to Nolie's arm, slowing her down a bit.

"It's a wee bit tricksy here," Bel said as the path began to wind downhill.

"Have you ever been ghost hunting before?" Nolie asked.

Bel's laugh was high and musical, just like the rest of her voice. "There aren't any ghosts in Journey's End," she said confidently. "We've had stories, just like every place 'round here. There used to be one about a ghost haunting a lighthouse."

She pointed out to sea, toward the Boundary. "Said she was a girl from the village who did . . . something bad, I don't recall what, and that as punishment, she was set adrift in a boat."

Nolie widened her eyes. "Whoa."

But Bel only shook her head. "It's not real," she said. "We don't even know if the bit about there being a *lighthouse* is real, much less a ghost."

She said it like even thinking there might be a ghost was the silliest thing in the world, and Nolie wondered why she'd agreed to come along. Maybe she'd just been bored in that little shop? "Do you work in your family's shop all the time?" Nolie asked, keeping her eyes on the ground in front of her.

Next to her, Bel nearly slid on some pebbles, but regained her footing quickly as she said, "In the summer, aye." She stopped, looking over at Nolie and brushing her hair back from her face. "I go to school during the year, you know," she added, like Nolie might be thinking they didn't even have school out here.

"I figured that," Nolie said, fidgeting with her sleeves. "But it's got to be kind of cool to have a job, right? Even during the summer? I've never had a summer job."

Bel started walking again and gave a little shrug. "Not really a *job*," she said. "Just ... helping out."

"Still," Nolie said, leaping over a bigger rock in the path, her arms held out at the side to keep her balance. "Better than how I spend my summers. My mom makes me go to, like, these day camps?" Now that she'd gotten the hang of jumping over the smaller rocks, she kept doing it, enjoying the way the salty wind lifted her jacket like wings.

"Oooh, camp," Bel said, and started jumping over the rocks, too. "I've always wanted to go to camp. Singing, fires, those treats with the marshmallows and chocolate."

"S'mores," Nolie offered. "And trust me, the camp I go to doesn't have those things. It's just making weird crafts in the community center."

Bel paused again, her head tilted to one side. "Well, in that case," she said, grinning at last, "no wonder you'd rather spend a summer ghost hunting."

Smiling back, Nolie nodded. "Exactly."

The path leveled out onto a rocky shore, and overhead, the sky was clearer.

"The rain stopped," she said, and the blond girl glanced over at her.

"That? That wasn't *rain*. It was mizzle."

When Nolie just started at her, Bel said, "Mist. Drizzle. Mix them together—"

"Mizzle," Nolie finished, nodding. "Got it. That's actually kind of a great word!"

Bel smiled again, and Nolie was suddenly really glad her dad had brought her into the village.

"My dad said there are caves here?" Nolie asked as they kept going down the path.

"Aye," Bel replied, kicking at a few stray pebbles. "Hundreds of 'em. No one even knows how many. My brother Simon used to tell me all sorts of scary stories about monsters living back there, or people who wandered in and never came back out."

"Is people disappearing even a scary thing when you live in Journey's End?" Nolie asked. She'd meant for it to be a joke, but Bel turned to her with a frown.

"'Course it is," she said, struggling to keep the wind from blowing her hair in her face. Nolie was glad she'd pulled her own hair back into a ponytail today. "Just because we're used to people goin' missing doesn't mean we *like* it."

Nolie wanted to offer an apology, but Bel was already turning and walking farther down the beach.

Nolie followed, careful of where she put her feet. The beaches she was used to were covered in sand, but this one was made up mostly of rocks. Some tiny, like the pebbles Bel was still kicking, and some huge boulders, covered with slippery orange algae.

Even through the rubber of her boots, Nolie could feel how cold the water was as it washed over her feet, and she curled her toes. Her dad had told her there were boats that took people out to the Boundary, but Nolie couldn't imagine wanting to sail out in this choppy gray water that looked like liquid rock.

"Here?" Bel called out, stopping at the base of a cliff. There was a cave to her back, a small one. Glancing up, Nolie could just make out the gabled roof of a house, and while she was pretty sure it was her dad's, all the houses on that cliff looked the same. "I think so," she hollered back.

Bel turned in a little half circle, looking around. "I don't see anyone."

Nolie joined her, on a flat slab of rock that reached out into the water, pointing at the Boundary like a finger.

It was true that the beach was deserted, and Nolie suddenly felt kind of stupid. Maybe she had just imagined the boy, and now she'd dragged Bel out here for nothing, and the one person she'd met so far—a person she actually liked—would think she was a total weirdo.

But Bel didn't seem to mind. "See that?" She pointed out at a white boat in the distance. "That's our boat. My dad and my brother are on it."

Nolie squinted, watching the vessel as it bobbed out toward the Boundary. "Are they fishermen?" she asked, and Bel laughed.

"Oh, no. Hardly anyone in Journey's End fishes anymore. It's a tour boat. You know, go out, look at the Boundary, take some pictures. That kind of thing."

Nolie looked more closely at the boat. "I get wanting to have a closer look, but I think I'd want a bigger boat?"

As soon as she'd said them, she wished she could call the words back, afraid she'd hurt Bel's feelings again.

But Bel only gave an easy shrug and said, "I don't get why any of the tourists want to do the stuff they do."

Nolie shoved her hands deeper in her pockets. "My dad is, like, obsessed with the Boundary. He always wanted to come here and work for the Institute and study it or whatever. If it were me, I'd be more interested in the people who disappeared, but he's studying . . . I don't know, its viscosity or some other science word. I'd want to know the *stories*, you know?" She looked at Bel. "There are stories, right?"

Bel dug into the pebbles with the tip of her boot. Her shoes, Nolie saw, were scuffed up and nearly the same dull greenish brown as the rocks under their feet. Nolie made a note to talk to her dad about getting her some less . . . colorful galoshes.

"Sure," Bel said, shoulders up by her ears against the wind. "About the people who went missing. And times when it seemed like the Boundary was moving closer . . . but they're just stories."

"But what happens in them?"

Another shrug. "Oh, you know. Village witch or someone like that says the fog is coming closer. Then a kid decides to be a hero and finds a spell or a talisman to save the day. There's a plaque in the city center about one of the legends. I'll show you when we get back."

"Okay, now we're talking," Nolie said. "Village witches, excellent. What else?"

"People say there's a lighthouse out there, too," Bel added, nodding out toward the ocean. "On a big rock you can barely call an island."

Haunted lighthouses? Even better, Nolie thought. "Is it lit?" she asked. The fog around where Bel was pointing was too thick to see anything.

Bel gave another shrug, the wind blowing her sandy

hair in her eyes. "Don't see how. No one can go out there, and there's no way to keep a lighthouse lamp going for so many years without any tending."

Smiling, Nolie looked back out at the fog. "Magic," she suggested, and Bel wrinkled her nose.

"Maybe," she said, but Nolie got the idea that she wasn't exactly a fan of the magical. Still, it had been nice of her to bring Nolie down here, even if ghosts and haunted lighthouses weren't really her thing.

Looking up the path they'd come from, Bel winced slightly. "I need to get to the shop. Mum's probably back from lunch by now."

"Sorry I dragged you out here for nothing," Nolie said, her face warm despite the biting wind. "I guess I was just imagining things. Wouldn't be the first time."

Bel waved that off. "You probably saw one of the lads from the village."

Nolie nodded, and turned to follow Bel back up the beach, but as she did, something caught her eye. At first, she thought it was the edge of another rock, but as she got closer, she could see that it was actually a little rowboat.

Nolie walked up to it, Bel trailing behind her. A few drops of rain had started to fall—real rain this time, not mizzle—and while Nolie grimaced and pulled the hood of her jacket up, Bel just stood there. Of course, Nolie thought, if you grew up in a place where it rained more often than not, a little rain probably wouldn't bother you.

"Someone lose a boat?" Nolie asked, and Bel shrugged.

"I've never seen that one before. And you'd have to be right out of your head to take something that old out on these waters." She nodded toward the sea, and Nolie crouched down closer to the boat.

It did look old. Really old, and the smell coming off it made her step back a little. There was a name painted on the side, a chipped black that still stood out against the faded gray of the boat.

"*The Selkie,*" Nolie read out loud, and Bel squatted down beside her.

"Good name for a boat," Bel observed, and Nolie reached out to run a finger over the letter S.

She was just about to tell Bel they should head back up to the village when Bel nodded toward the base of the cliff. There, in the tiny strip of sand that ran alongside the rock, were a few footprints, clearly made by bare feet.

There were five prints that Nolie could see, the hollows already filling with water. The boy she'd seen had his pants rolled up, hadn't he? The more she thought about it, the more she was sure he'd been barefooted.

"So there *was* someone out here," Bel mused.

Nolie felt her heart leap. *Settle down,* she reminded herself. *You don't want this girl thinking you're a complete weirdo.*

"I guess," she replied, trying to sound casual. "But probably one of the kids from your village. Like you said."

Bel squinted at the tracks, her blond hair blowing all around her heart-shaped face. And then she nodded at where the prints disappeared, just inside the mouth of one of the caves.

"Let's find out."

CHAPTER 5

NOLIE STOOD ON THE BEACH, WATCHING BEL DISAPPEAR
into the mouth of the cave.

"We're just going right in?" she asked. "Wow, y'all are
really tough in Scotland."

Bel's head popped back out of the cave. Screwing up
her face, she asked, "Did you just say 'y'all'? I didn't know
that was a thing people actually said."

"I didn't think Scottish people actually said 'aye' or
'wee,' but you do," Nolie reminded her, and Bel laughed.

"Fair enough. So are you coming? I have a torch."

Once again, Nolie just blinked at her. "Like . . . a stick
on fire?"

Grinning, Bel reached into her jacket and pulled out
a key ring, clicking the button on a little flashlight attached to it. It didn't give much light, but it was better
than nothing, Nolie guessed.

"It's not a ghost," Bel told her. "Ghosts don't have footprints."

"No, but serial killers do," Nolie replied. "Which is why this seems like the *real* kind of scary."

Bel tilted her head to one side, looking at Nolie with that whole wrinkled-nose thing she'd done before. "Ghosts aren't the real kind of scary?"

Shaking her head, Nolie dug her hands deeper into her pockets and said, "No, ghosts are the *fun* kind of scary. The fun kind of scary is . . . I don't know, like when you're inside your house on a stormy day. Nothing can actually hurt you, you know? The *real* kind of scary is the sort of thing where you end up on the news or *CSI: Whatever.*"

"CSI?" Bel asked, and Nolie sighed, waving her off.

"It's a cop show. But . . . okay, we'll go check it out, I guess."

She followed Bel into the cave. There was a hole somewhere high up in the rock that let thin, watery light through, enough so they didn't really need Bel's flashlight. There wasn't much to the cave, and it didn't go back very far. It was more like a big, round room with a little shelf of rock jutting out from one wall.

"It's not that scary, really," Nolie offered, and Bel turned off her "torch," putting the key ring back in her pocket.

"Not really," she agreed. "Except I think this was the cave Bluidy George was said to live in."

When Nolie just looked at her, Bel tucked her hair behind her ears. "He was a murderer in the fourteen hundreds. Hid in caves and murdered people."

Nolie screwed up her face, thinking. "That's in a weird place between *fun* scary and *real* scary."

"Then he ate them."

"That doesn't really help," Nolie said, and Bel's teeth flashed white in the gloom.

"Sorry."

"But no ghost, at least," Nolie said. "And no serial killer, either. Unless Bloody George is still around."

"Bluidy," Bel corrected, and Nolie tried again. The word felt weird in her mouth, the same way *Caillte* had, and embarrassed, she shoved her hands into her pockets.

"The accent is going to take a while, I guess."

Bel turned to face Nolie, her hands in her own pockets. "Y'all," she said, and it didn't sound like the way Nolie said it at all. It was all stretched out, and Bel kind of rolled her Ls at the end, making Nolie grin.

With a dramatic sigh, Bel lifted her shoulders. "We'll *both* have to practice."

Nolie turned to look around. The walls of the cave were damp, and the sand under her boots squelched as she walked forward, looking up at the opening in the rock. It struck her that Journey's End was a pretty gray place. Gray rocks, gray buildings, gray water, even gray sky.

And the gray fog.

Thinking about it, Nolie decided that she wanted to keep her purple galoshes after all. It seemed like Journey's End needed more purple.

"Thanks for bringing me here," Nolie said, looking back over at Bel. "Even if you don't believe in ghosts."

Bel gave a little shrug and her face went pink. "Seemed like a good way to welcome you to Journey's End."

Nolie nodded. "Definitely. Ghost hunting on my first day? What was that word you used about the book? *Ace.*"

That made Bel smile, too, and Nolie was going to ask if they could hang out more the next day when a strange noise came from behind her.

It sounded almost like the patter of footsteps on stone, faint but echoing in the cave.

Next to her, Bel tensed up, too, looking around.

"There's no one in here but us," she said, but Nolie didn't think Bel sounded convinced.

Almost at the same time, they saw the opening in the wall. Thanks to the dim light inside the cave, it was nearly invisible, and unless you were staring right at it, the passage just looked like a discoloration in the rock. But it was an opening, stretching who knew how far back, and as Nolie stared at it, the sound of footsteps still echoing, the hair on the back of her neck stood up.

"Bel?" she asked, and the other girl lifted her chin, squaring her shoulders.

"I know that's you, Donal McLeod," she called, her voice wavering only a little bit. "Or one of your stupid friends, and you can't scare us."

There was no answer, but Nolie swore she could hear the faintest sawing of breath.

Moving a little closer to Bel, she whispered, "Would it be okay if we just ran away now?"

Bel nodded vigorously. "Yes, let's."

They ran out of the cave with shrieking laughs, their hands clutching at each other's arms, and Nolie's heart was hammering as they skidded to a stop there at the surf, but she was giggling, her fingers still tight on Bel's jacket.

"Sorry I almost got you murdered on your first day," Bel panted, and Nolie laughed even though she was a little breathless herself.

"It's cool. The heart attack definitely took my mind off my jet lag."

Bel giggled again before letting go of Nolie's arm and hopping up on a nearby rock. But as soon as she did, she skidded back a little, her smile fading, and Nolie hopped up next to her to see what was wrong.

Just a little bit down the beach, she could make out

four people. There were three girls—two with dark hair, one with hair almost as red as Nolie's—and a boy.

A boy with nearly black hair, just like the boy she'd seen on the beach.

"That's Donal," Bel said, her voice oddly flat now. "I bet that's who you saw."

"Probably," Nolie agreed, even if she didn't really think it was. This Donal guy was wearing a jersey with some kind of mascot emblazoned on it, and jeans, not the old-fashioned clothes the boy she'd seen had been wearing.

Bel was watching the girls more than the boy, though, and she seemed to almost shrink into herself as they looked over at her and Nolie.

"Are those girls your friends?" Nolie asked, and Bel shook her head.

"No. I mean . . . kind of? One of them used to be."

Nolie knew that feeling. There had been a girl in fourth grade, Caroline, who'd been her best friend—until suddenly, one day, she wasn't.

The girls were talking together, too far away to overhear, but their laughter carried over, high-pitched and grating.

Nolie found herself scowling at all of them, but they were already turning to walk back down the beach, and Bel was looking out to the ocean.

She shaded her eyes even though the sun still hadn't broken through the clouds, looking out toward the Boundary. That white boat she'd said was her family's was barely more than a speck now. "Dad'll be out another hour at least," she said with a sigh.

Then she toed at the damp sand and rocks. "So how long has your dad worked at the Institute?" Bel asked, her eyes still on the boat in the distance.

"About six months," Nolie answered, and it was on the tip of her tongue to tell Bel that her parents were divorced, and one of the big reasons for that was that her dad wanted to live here in Scotland and her mom hadn't wanted to. But she'd just met this girl, and good taste in books or not, she wasn't sure that was the kind of thing you just told people.

Instead, she turned her back to the water, facing Bel, and said, "I'm actually supposed to go to the Institute with him tomorrow. Do you wanna . . . I mean, if you're not busy, you could come, too."

"Up to the Institute?"

The word "to" sounded more like "ta" to Nolie, and it made her smile. "Yeah."

Bel chewed her lower lip, still staring out at the sea. "Never been to the Institute," she said at last. "No one in the village has, far as I know."

Nolie blinked, her hands moving a little deeper into

her pockets. "That seems weird. I mean, it's been here for-ever, right?"

With a nod, Bel hopped off the rock she was standing on, her boots sliding in the pebbles. "Yeah, but the two things have always been separate. Institute up there"—she raised a hand toward the cliffs above them—"village down here." Lowering her palm, Bel held it out at her waist.

Nolie worried a stray pebble with the toe of her boot. "My dad said that people in the village aren't happy with the Institute right now," she offered, and Bel nodded.

"Oh, aye. Last week, they wanted to fly these wee robot things into the Boundary?"

"Drones?" Nolie suddenly thought her dad's work might be cooler than she'd thought.

"That's it," Bel said, looking back out at the Boundary. "Drones. Anyway, no one in Journey's End really wanted them to do it, though. Not sure why, just that it was 'tampering with things,' or something like that. There was a petition and everything."

Suddenly those dirty looks her dad had gotten in town made more sense. "But the Institute did it anyway?" she asked, already knowing the answer.

Bel confirmed it with another nod. "Aye. Few days back now." She shrugged, tucking her hair behind her ears. "Not sure what all the fuss was, though. Anyway, I'd like to see the Institute. I'll have to ask my mum."

"She didn't sign the petition?" Nolie joked, but Bel looked back at her, a deep V between her brows.

"She wrote it."

CHAPTER 6

"SO WHERE WERE YOU THIS AFTERNOON?"

Bel looked up from her book to see her mum leaning in the doorway. Like Bel, she had blond hair, although hers had gone darker as she'd gotten older. She also had Bel's small nose, which made Bel feel better every time she looked in the mirror and thought she looked a bit puggish. *Not puggish*, she'd remind herself. *Like Mum*.

Her mum was looking down that nose at her now. Bel dog-eared her page, laying the book next to her on the bed. "I went down to the beach. I knew you'd be coming right back, so—"

Mum cut her off with a shake of her head. "Not worried about the shop being closed. Town was deserted anyway. It's just that it's not like you to leave in the middle of the afternoon."

Bel didn't answer right away, and her mum sat on the edge of her bed, the mattress sinking slightly.

"I saw Leslie and her friends when I was headed back

from lunch," Mum said, her voice soft. "Did they come in the store?"

Bel rolled her shoulders, uncomfortable. "Just for a second."

Sighing, Mum reached out and ruffled Bel's hair. "I know it's rough fighting with friends, love."

Bel didn't bother telling Mum that she and Leslie hadn't actually *had* a fight. Sometimes she wished something big and dramatic had happened, like they did on the soaps her nan watched.

Then, at least, there would've been a thing to point to. *Proof* of why Leslie didn't seem to like her anymore.

Instead of saying any of that, Bel said, "I met this girl. Her dad works for the Institute and she's in town for the summer." Bel scooted back against her headboard, circling her knees with her arms. "She seemed nice."

She didn't add that she'd taken Nolie down to the beach and the caves in search of a ghost. Not that she believed in ghosts, of course. Like she'd said to Nolie, it was probably Donal. He was dark-haired, and definitely the type to be messing about in those caves. But she'd liked Nolie's bright smile and purple wellies so much, and if ghost hunting would help make them friends, Bel had been willing to give it a shot.

Mum reached out to tuck a strand of Bel's hair behind her ear. "That's brilliant, Bonny Bel," she said, but her face didn't seem to think it was brilliant. There was a crease between her brows, and her eyes were slightly narrowed.

"I know you don't like me spending time with the tourists—" Bel began, but Mum shook her head.

"It's not that I don't like it. I just want you to understand that friendships with outsiders can be ... difficult."

Bel nodded. It was the same talk Mum always gave, the one most kids in Journey's End received from their parents at some point. The village was so small that visitors were always exciting, even though they came every summer. But that's all they were: visitors. And kids born in Journey's End tended to stay in Journey's End, while the visitors almost always left. Nearly every family had a story about someone whose heart had been broken after the tourist they'd fallen in love with had left and forgotten all about them.

Friendships were just as dangerous, according to Bel's mum, who began listing the reasons as she folded her long legs to sit on Bel's bed. "It's just that it's so hard to stay in touch when people leave here, Bel."

"I know," Bel said on a sigh, glancing over at the laptop on her desk. She'd inherited it from Simon, who'd gotten a new one when he'd gone off to uni, but it wasn't good for much besides typing. Journey's End *technically* got the internet, but just like the TV and mobile phones, it never worked exactly right. Bel didn't even have an email address, much less a Facebook, or her own YouTube channel, or a blog. There had never been a point. She saw the same kids every day at school, and those were the same kids she'd seen at school the year before. The same kids she'd been seeing since nursery school, really. So what was the point of seeing them online, too? If anything interesting happened, she'd hear about it at school.

But that's what made it hard to find friends who lived outside the village. Other kids did have Facebooks and email addresses and mobile phones that worked. And when they couldn't get in touch with people in Journey's End by using those methods, they tended to stop trying to contact the friends they'd made on vacation.

It was what every kid in Journey's End grew up learning; eventually, the outlanders would only hurt you.

"She's not here on holiday, really," Bel said to her mum. "If her dad lives here, maybe she'll come every summer."

"Maybe," Mum agreed, but again, Bel could see that she didn't really believe it.

For a moment, Bel thought about pointing out to her mum that it wasn't only the visitors to Journey's End who could hurt you. She'd known Leslie her whole life, and look how that had gone.

Of course, that all might have been because of Alice, which would just prove Mum's point.

Bel sighed. Why did every kind of friendship have to be so hard?

Folding her arms, Mum looked around Bel's room. It was little, not much more than a closet, really, with the low ceilings and shadowy corners that came from being tucked under the eaves of the house.

Bel loved it. As the only girl in a house full of brothers, she'd been given her own room, and even though it was tiny and dim and so close to the washer that every time Mum did laundry, Bel's bed vibrated, it was *hers*. But then she thought about how a girl like Nolie might see this room—Nolie, who lived in one of the big houses and wore new wellies with daisies on them.

"She invited me to go with her to the Institute to-morrow," Bel said, and Mum's head jerked toward her.

"The Institute?"

"Her dad wanted to show her around, and she asked if I'd come with her." Bel sat up a little straighter. "Can I go?"

Mum's shoulders rose and fell beneath her plaid shirt, and Bel thought she might be about to say she couldn't go. Bel didn't get told no very often, but then, she hardly ever asked for anything. With three boys in the house, the McKissicks usually had their hands full. And that usually suited Bel just fine—she didn't mind life in the background.

Mum finally patted Bel's knee and said, "Just don't stay gone too long. Are they picking you up at the shop?"

"Yeah."

Mum nodded. "All right. But I want to meet them before you go."

"Done," Bel said with a grin, and her mum smiled, too, reaching out to tap the end of Bel's nose.

"Have to admit," Mum said as she got off the bed, "I'm a bit jealous. I've always wanted to see the inside of that place."

Bel thought of the Institute, a big, old house converted to a lab years and years ago. She'd always stayed away from it—everyone in Journey's End did—but she'd always been curious, too. And now she would finally get to see it. Get a tour, even.

She wasn't sure whether she was excited or nervous. A bit of both, really.

Mum walked to the one small, round window high up on the far wall. It was another part of the room Bel loved. Made her feel like she was on a ship, looking out a porthole.

"Your brother said something about the Boundary feeling funny today," Mum told her, crossing her arms as she looked out. You could barely make out the Caillte Sea from their house—it was just a smudge of gray in the distance—and you could never see the Boundary, since their house didn't face it, but Bel liked the view anyway.

"It's a magical fog bank, Mum," Bel teased. "It's *meant* to feel funny."

Her mum turned back, tugging at the hem of her shirt. "Hardly magic, silly. It's just . . ." she trailed off, sighing. "I just wish the Institute hadn't gone mucking about with those little remote control robots."

"Drones," Bel supplied, and her mum nodded.

"Aye, those. Flying drones into it, taking pictures, when the whole point of the tourist boats is 'the closest look you'll ever get at the Boundary.'" She snorted softly, folding her arms. "Probably didn't even *read* the petition. And I doubt a one of those drones came back." She shook her head. "Waste of time all around."

Bel shifted on her bed, tugging her Midlothian Hearts blanket up over her knees. "Not a *total* waste, though, right? Doing science? Figuring it all out?"

Bel's mum made a noise in her throat that sounded like she wasn't so sure about that. "Just doesn't seem like a thing people should be messing about with," she said at last, and Bel picked her book back up.

"Tell you what, Mum. Tomorrow, when I go to the Institute, if I see any machines that say 'Fog Mucker-Upper,' I will sabotage them."

That made Mum laugh, and as she walked past the bed,

she ruffled Bel's hair again. "You do that, my wee mad scientist," she teased, but before she left, Bel caught another glimpse of her face.

Mum usually looked worried—having three sons, and a husband whose job it was to take a boat out toward a thing that *eats* boats, will do that—but there was something different in her expression now.

She almost looked . . . scared.

FROM "THE SAD TALE OF CAIT MCINNISH,"
CHAPTER 13,
Legends of the North

AN ACCIDENT. A HORRIBLE ONE, OF COURSE, BUT AN accident all the same. Cait had loved little Rabbie as though he were her own, had been his nanny since he was barely out of the cradle, and if she could've taken his place on his funeral bower, she would have.

Cait could not trade her life for Rabbie's, but that did not mean the laird of the castle would let her live.

The girl who did not believe in magic was condemned as a witch, the laird claiming she had purposely thrown his son, his heir, from the tall tower to imbue herself with power.

Cait was a girl from the village, and she waited for the village to rise to her defense. They knew she was no witch. They knew Rabbie's death was a tragedy, but not a murder.

The village stayed quiet, though. And when Cait sat in a bottle dungeon in the laird's castle, her knees drawn to her chest, her breathing even louder than the waves that crashed outside, the village remained quiet. And when the laird announced his punishment—that Cait would be put in a rowboat and left to die in the middle of the Caillte Sea—the village went quieter still.

Perhaps they were not staying silent, but merely holding their breath, hoping for the laird's grief and rage to pass, hoping it could all be vented onto this one girl and not at them. This girl who had been one of them until her fourteenth birthday, when she'd gone to work in the castle on the hill.

CHAPTER 7

"WHY IS THERE FISH ON THE TABLE?" NOLIE ASKED, staring at what was apparently breakfast.

Her dad turned away from the coffeepot to grin at her.

"Kippers," he said. "Thought you might want a traditional Scottish breakfast for your first morning here."

Pulling out a chair, Nolie kept her eyes on that row of skinny fish, their heads still on. The kitchen was small, without room for much more than the table and a refrigerator a lot smaller than the one Nolie had back home in Georgia. Outside, it was gray again, a soft rain pattering against the windows.

"Come on, Nol," her dad said, picking up his coffee cup and taking the seat opposite her. "If you can do grits, you can do kippers."

Nolie wanted to point out that there was a big difference between a nice bowl of grits—preferably with lots of shredded cheese—and a fried fish that was *still looking at her*, but hey, she was here to try new things, right?

So Nolie put a kipper on her plate, along with a grilled tomato, cooked mushrooms, two pieces of toast, and a slab of something her dad *said* was bacon, but looked more like regular ham to her.

"Did you make all this?" she asked, putting butter on her toast.

Dad leaned back in his chair. "Yup," he said. "I've gotten pretty good at the full Scottish, although I did leave out the beans."

Beans? Nolie shuddered, pushing her mushrooms around the plate. But even if the breakfast wasn't what she was used to, she was weirdly relieved her dad had made it. Looking at that spread, it occurred to her that he might have a girlfriend, some Scottish lady who cooked for him and stood over his shoulder while he worked at his computer. Someone he walked through the village with, hand in hand.

Nolie told herself she would've been fine if that was the case—her mom had been out on two dates since the divorce, and that hadn't been so bad—but still, it was nicer to think of her dad in here by himself, making this breakfast for her because he wanted to share something Scottish he liked.

And that's why Nolie ate not one, not two, but *three* bites of the kipper.

Once breakfast was done, she and her dad got into his

car, heading out to pick up Bel so they could bring her to the Institute.

Dad stopped at the mailbox on their way down the drive, and as soon as Nolie saw the bright purple envelope in his hand, she grinned, making grabby hands at him. "Gimme, gimme," she said, making him laugh as he got back in the car and handed her the letter from her mom.

"I take it you were expecting this?"

"Mom said she was sending one before I even left," Nolie explained. "I think she was hoping it would get here before I did."

She went to open the letter, but then looked over at her dad. He was driving again, eyes on the road, and even though she knew it wouldn't have hurt his feelings or anything if she read the letter from her mom—and she really, really wanted to read it—she decided to save it for later, when she was alone.

The drive to the village was short, and Nolie twisted in her seat, looking back up the hill they'd come down. "I bet I could walk that pretty easy," she said, and her dad nodded.

"Just about everything in the village is within walking distance," he told her. "It's just that the weather is usually so bad, people prefer to drive."

Nolie settled back into her seat. That was good to

know. She didn't like the idea of being dependent on Dad every time she wanted to do anything.

Bel and her mum were standing outside the store as they pulled up, and Nolie didn't miss the way Bel's mum's eyebrows drew together as she looked at Dad.

"Dr. Stanhope," she said when Dad got out of the car, and he gave her a smile in return.

"Mrs. McKissick," he replied. "Thank you for letting Bel spend the day with Nolie. I think they really hit it off yesterday."

"*Dad*," Nolie said in a low voice, but she smiled at Bel and gave her a little wave.

Bel returned it, but Nolie thought she might be picking up on the tension between their parents, too.

"Just . . . have her back by four?" Bel's mum said, giving Bel's shoulders a little squeeze, and Nolie's dad touched the brim of his hat in a salute.

"Will do," he said, and then Bel got into the backseat. Nolie did, too, wanting to sit beside her rather than up front.

"I'm glad this morning is starting off super awkward," she said, and to her relief, Bel started laughing.

"So, scale of one to Loch Ness monster, what's creepier, that cave or this place?"

Nolie asked the question about an hour later as she

attempted to slide down a banister, but the tights she'd had to wear underneath her shorts—seriously, this place was way too cold for June—snagged on the wood, and she nearly tipped off and onto the stairs.

From the landing above her, Bel laughed and gave her own slide down the banister. "Oh, cave, definitely. This place isn't creepy; it's just old."

"Old *and* creepy," Nolie argued, jumping down. As if agreeing with her, the floorboards beneath her feet creaked loudly, and when Bel finished her slide, there was a thick layer of dust across her backside. She swiped at it as Nolie sighed and leaned back against a nearby bookcase.

So far, their trip to her dad's work had been less than thrilling. He said he'd give them a tour, but as soon as they came in, one of his assistants told him there were some readings he needed to look at. Dad sighed at that, but when he turned back to Nolie and Bel, he seemed fairly cheerful, telling them they could explore the Institute. "All the equipment we use now is on the ground floor," he told them, "but there's still some neat stuff to see upstairs."

Nolie wasn't sure she and her dad had the same idea of what kind of stuff was "neat." The second floor was dim and dusty, and most of the doors were locked. The one Nolie and Bel had been able to be open was filled with stuffed animals. And not like the sheep they sold at Bel's shop. Actual animals, stuffed and preserved, their glass eyes glittering in the gloom.

Bel and Nolie had closed that door pretty fast.

The third floor was better, though. There was a room with big tables covered in old maps, and another filled with different species of plants growing under glass domes. A third room held old equipment the Institute no longer used, and that's where Bel and Nolie had decided to stay for a while.

The room was technically two levels, with a small staircase that led up to a wide platform in front of giant floor-to-ceiling windows. There were a couple of old telescopes set up there, and Nolie jogged back up the stairs to look through one of the brass eyepieces. The lens was greasy with age and disuse, and all Nolie could see outside was gray anyway. Gray sky, gray water, gray fog. Same as yesterday.

"Why even *have* a telescope pointed at the Boundary?" Nolie asked. "Does it ever change?"

"Not really," Bel replied. "My brother said it felt 'funny' yesterday, but I have no idea what that meant."

Nolie kept her eye pressed to the eyepiece, looking out at the waves. "Maybe I could get a job here. Keeping an eye on the fog. Today it seems gray. Yesterday it was also gray, and I'm thinking that tomorrow, there's a good chance of gray."

"Partial chance of 'more grayish than usual,'" Bel added, and Nolie nodded.

"We are *killing it* at this fog watching job. They should give us at least ten pounds a week. However much that is."

Bel's lips quirked up, and Nolie kept looking through the telescope, tilting it this way and that, not that she actually expected to see anything.

"Is your dad taking the boat out today?" she asked.

She could hear Bel sit down behind her, probably on the edge of the platform, if the drumming of her heels was any clue.

"Not sure. Depends if anyone shows up. And Mum wanted Jaime to do some chores around the house today."

Straightening, Nolie glanced over at Bel. She was indeed sitting on the edge of the platform, looking down, her sandy hair sliding forward so that Nolie could just see the tip of her nose.

"How many brothers do you have?" she asked, and Bel looked up, blinking.

"Three. Simon's at uni, though, so just two in the house. Jaime's seventeen, and Jack's five. I'm piggy in the middle."

That made Nolie laugh, even though the idea of having *three brothers* kind of blew her mind.

"There's just me in my family," she told Bel. "Lone piggy, I guess."

Now it was Bel's turn to laugh, and she tilted her

head, looking at Nolie curiously. "Do you wish you had brothers or sisters?"

Nolie did actually feel like a lonely piggy some of the time, but she also really liked the peace that came with knowing no one was going to come barging into her room. "Can't really miss something you've never had," she said.

"Suppose that's true," Bel said, nodding.

"Besides, it was nice, just the three of us," Nolie added. "Like a team."

Now *that* she did miss, the three of them sitting around the dinner table, joking over pizza. The way she'd felt on long car trips, sitting in the backseat and listening to her parents chat in the front. How, when she was little, they'd each hold one of her hands and lift her up between them as they walked down the sidewalk.

Bel leaned back and thought that over. "I think that's how my dad and my brothers feel sometimes," she said. "Simon and Jaime love the boat like my dad does, even if Simon is off at school now. And maybe my mum feels like that with Jack, since she's home with him so much." Bel shrugged. "S'pose I don't really have a team in my family."

"Neither do I anymore, I guess," Nolie said, and then felt like maybe she'd said too much, or given something away.

She thought Bel might feel the same, because she

cleared her throat and said, "Anyway, if you ever *do* find yourself missing out, you can come to my house. I can promise that you won't want any siblings after that."

Nolie patted the cracked leather case of the telescope. "I'd like that. Going to your house, I mean."

Bel smiled. "So would I. We could even have a sleepover, maybe! Haven't had one of those in ages."

"Awesome," Nolie said, and she swung the telescope away from the sea, toward the other window that looked out over the cliffs.

Nolie adjusted the focus, and after a second, she could see a massive stone building sitting on a bright green hill. "Oooh, I can see a castle!" she said. "That's way better than fog."

Bel walked up next to Nolie, her boots clomping. She was wearing those greenish-brown wellies she'd had on yesterday, and Nolie wondered if people just wore them all the time.

Nolie moved back so Bel could look.

"That's not a castle," Bel said. "There used to be a castle there, but it's all ruins now. See? Those lumps of stone?"

She lifted her head and gestured for Nolie to take a look. Nolie did, and once again saw the giant house, which certainly looked castle-y to *her*, but then, Bel would be the expert. This must be the house her dad had mentioned on her first day—the "old manor house."

Nolie looked a little closer, and sure enough, there were mounds of gray stones littering the green hillside.

"It was struck by lightning a really long time ago," Bel said. "Gutted the whole place, so the family that was living there left and built that big house to live in instead."

"Ruins of a lightning-struck castle?" Nolie said, her eyes going wide. "Okay, yes, we are so totally checking that out. That has got to be *suuuuper* haunted."

Bel laughed again, shaking her head. "It's just old rocks, Nolie."

Scoffing, Nolie looked back through the telescope. "Where is your imagination, Bel? Do you think it was struck by lightning because of a curse? Ooh, or maybe there was, like, a *witch* or something, trying to do a big spell and, BOOM, lightning!"

"I think there was a storm and lightning struck the tallest building, which happened to be a castle," Bel said.

Nolie tilted the telescope a little so she could get a better view of the big house that was *not* a castle. "You sound like my dad," she said to Bel. "Very science-y. Who lives in that big house now?"

Bel had moved away again, and when Nolie looked up, she was standing by the window that faced the Boundary.

"Mrs. McLeod," she said. "Really old lady, been in Journey's End for donkey's years."

Nolie studied the back of her head. "Is that a long time?"

Bel turned back, crossing her arms over her chest. "The longest time. It's like she's always been here. She hardly ever comes down to the village, though."

"So you're telling me you have magic fog, a haunted ruined castle, *and* a creepy old lady living in a big house on a hill?" Shaking her head, Nolie gave Bel a mock-stern look. "Girl, you have been holding out on me."

Again, Bel just shrugged that off. "She's not creepy; she's just old. And no one wants to bother her, because she keeps to herself. Plus, Mum thinks she's the 'anonymous benefactor' who contributes to the town fund every year, so best to keep her happy."

Nolie nodded and turned the telescope. "That makes sense. Guess I should stop spying on her, then."

Once the lens was pointed at the Boundary again, she looked back out at it. "Maybe they were keeping an eye out for people who came back. Like my new BFF, Albert."

She'd meant it as a joke, but a little wrinkle appeared between Bel's brows.

"You didn't see Albert," she said.

Nolie nodded. She'd been so sure the boy she saw on the beach was the same boy on the back wall of Bel's family's shop, and almost without thinking, she tilted the telescope back down toward the beach.

She heard Bel get up, felt her come to stand by her elbow.

"Do you see anything?" Bel whispered, and suddenly Nolie wondered if Bel was as much of an unbeliever as she'd claimed.

"I don't see—" Nolie started, but before she could finish, there was a flash of movement on the beach. Just a blur of dark hair and white shirt, moving over the rocks and toward the cave.

Nolie's heart hammered hard against her ribs, and she stepped back from the telescope, eyes wide. "Someone's down there."

CHAPTER 8

THE RAIN WAS LIGHTER AS BEL LED THE WAY BACK DOWN to the beach. She was still more than a little surprised Nolie's dad had let them go, but when Nolie had asked to walk Bel back to her family's shop, he'd been distracted reading something on his computer. "Try not to drown," he'd called after them, and Nolie had laughed, even as the very word *drown* made Bel's blood feel cold.

Only people who didn't have the sea in their veins could make jokes about a thing like that.

Nolie was in her bright purple wellies again, and Bel's own sensible greens nearly slid on the slick pebbles once they reached the shore. She and Nolie hadn't talked much on their way here, but Bel got the idea that, to Nolie, this was all a bit of a laugh. Tromping down the beach to see a ghost. Nolie had grabbed a notebook out of her room—a big, airy space nothing like Bel's little attic nook—before she'd left. It was black, covered in bright pink skulls, and when Bel glanced at it, Nolie just said, "For observations."

They were nearly to the caves now, Nolie almost skipping ahead, the fear she'd felt yesterday clearly gone, and Bel trudged on, curious despite herself.

The rain had stopped altogether now, and Nolie shoved the hood of her rain slicker up as she studied the caves in front of them, tipping her head back to look up the cliff. They couldn't see the Institute from here, but Bel knew Nolie was trying to work out her bearings. "I think it was this one?" she said, nodding at a slightly smaller cave than the one they'd gone into the day before.

"You said he was down there yesterday," Bel reminded Nolie, gesturing a little ways down the beach, but Nolie shook her head.

"No, he went in this one today."

And with that, she stepped forward, leaving Bel no choice but to follow.

As soon as she did, she could see why someone might choose this cave to hide in. It wasn't as big as the other one, but it was darker, and she moved a little closer to Nolie. "It's a prank," she said, keeping her voice low. "I'm sure of it. We should go back."

Nolie turned to her, confused. "You came with me yesterday," she reminded Bel. "I thought . . . I guess I thought you liked it?"

Bel didn't know how to explain that she'd only gone along because she thought *Nolie* would like it. And if this were some kind of stupid prank, what if it made Nolie think Bel might not be someone she wanted to be friends with after all?

"It's just—" she started, and then she froze.

There was a sound from the back of the cave. A rustle, a slight intake of breath, and Bel slowly turned to see a figure standing just a few feet away.

Nolie saw him at the same time; a little shriek escaped her lips, and both girls stood there like their feet had been glued to the ground.

The boy stood against the back wall of the cave, a piece of driftwood held in one hand, lifted over his head. In the dim light of the cave, it was impossible to see much except that he was only a little taller than Bel herself, close to Nolie's height. He was more a collection of shapes and shadows, and for all that Bel had teased Nolie about ghosts and monsters back here in these sea caves, she suddenly felt her throat go tight with fear.

"Stay back!" he warned. "I'll dash yer brains out, see if I won't!" For all his bold words, he didn't sound confident in his brain-dashing skills, and there was something about his voice that struck Bel as odd. He was clearly Scottish like her, but his accent was thicker, less familiar than the voices she heard every day.

Maybe he was from Glasgow?

"Okay, easy, dude," Nolie said, holding her hands up in front of her. Bel was impressed with how calm she sounded, but then, Nolie was American, so maybe this wasn't the first time she'd had to deal with crazy people threatening to kill her.

"There's no need for anyone to dash anything," Nolie said. "We were just looking around the caves, and we'll go now."

"Ye do that," the boy said, shaking the piece of drift-wood for good measure.

Bel tugged at Nolie's jacket. "Yeah, let's do that."

They backed up together, Bel's fingers still tight around Nolie's sleeve, their eyes on the boy in front of them. They were nearly to the mouth of the cave when the boy moved forward—just a little bit, but enough so that the light fell on his face, and Bel could see him clearly.

And when she did, her fingers fell from Nolie's sleeve, suddenly feeling bloodless and numb.

"Al?" she asked, and he moved farther into the light.

There was no doubt in her mind that this was indeed Albert MacLeish, the boy she'd stared at on the back wall of her parents' shop all her life. He was dressed in a dingy white shirt, a brown waistcoat over that, and brown trousers. His feet were bare and pale, which meant he had to be *freezing*. Bel could feel the damp through her shoes, after all. Being barefoot here would be painful, but he didn't seem to notice.

He frowned at her, but dropped the arm at his side a fraction, his brow wrinkling with confusion. "How do you know my name?"

"We saw you yesterday," Nolie said, giving Bel a look that clearly said, *I told you so.* "And also, you're one of the dead people on the back wall of her family's shop."

"I'm not dead!" Al insisted, his voice a bit shrill.

"Then you're a ghost," Nolie said, practically bouncing up and down on the balls of her feet. "An *actual ghost*, not even on night vision or *anything*." Then she stopped bouncing, studying Al with her head tilted to one side a bit. "Or maybe you're a zombie?"

Al was looking more and more freaked out, his gaze darting around, his hands clenching and unclenching in fists, and Bel decided it was time she stepped in.

"The boat was yours, wasn't it?" she asked Al, taking a hesitant step forward. "The *Selkie*? We found her the other day. So you must've used it to come back from the Boundary, which sounds mad—"

"It *is* mad," Nolie interrupted, "if we're using that to mean 'crazy.' But that's why this is all so *great*."

Through all of this, Al was very quiet, watching them. He wasn't wielding the branch anymore, which Bel thought was a good sign.

"What year is it?" she asked him. "I mean, what year was it when you went into the Boundary?"

Al waited so long to answer that Bel was afraid he wouldn't say anything at all. But then he sniffed and said, "1918."

Nolie blew out a long, shaky breath, and Bel felt like she'd just swallowed a whole net of butterflies. "So you *are* a ghost," Bel said, and Albert stepped forward quickly, one finger pointing at her.

"I am no—" he began, and then his words ended in a hiss of pain.

He looked down, and Bel followed his gaze. Al had stubbed his big toe on one of the sharp rocks that littered the floor of the cave, and a bright line of red blood welled out from its tip.

"Um. I have read a lot of books about ghosts, and while I'm not an *expert*, I *am* pretty sure they don't bleed," Nolie said, breaking the silence.

"That's fine. I'm not a ghost," Al said, still sounding cross even as he sat down to inspect the cut.

"Then I'm right and you're a zombie, which, in my book, is actually creepier." Nolie turned back to Bel. "Has anything like this ever happened before? Someone coming back from the Boundary?"

There were a few spooky stories in those books that Nolie liked, saying that once a year, people who had been lost to the Boundary could come back to walk the beaches at night, things like that. Just scary tales for the tourists, nothing real.

"It's impossible," Bel said. "People don't ... not-grow-up for a hundred years."

"A hundred years?"

They looked back to the rock where Al was sitting, and now he was staring at them, dark eyes wide. "That's how long I've been gone?"

Bel's mouth felt dry, and she realized she had no idea what to say to him. How would it feel to come back to a world where everyone you knew was long dead? Your friends? Your family? But no, he *couldn't* be over a hundred years old, because that was impossible, and Bel McKissick did *not* believe in impossible things.

But she didn't have to say anything, because Al suddenly shot to his feet, and with a scrabble of pebbles and something like a sob, ran off into the darkness.

CHAPTER 9

NOLIE STARED AT THE SPOT WHERE THE BOY HAD DIS-appeared, then stepped toward the back of the cave.

Bel caught her sleeve and tugged slightly. "Let him go," she said. "If we follow, he might rethink bashing our brains out."

Nolie stopped, looking in the direction where Albert had gone. "But I didn't even write anything down in my notebook!" she argued. "And besides, he's not that big. Plus, if he *isn't* a ghost, he's like a hundred and something years old. I bet we could take him."

That made Bel laugh, even though Nolie hadn't really been joking. That kid looked like he weighed as much as a third grader, all skinny arms and legs, and Nolie hadn't taken tae kwon do for nothing.

Still, she followed Bel out of the cave and back onto the beach. Not only had the rain stopped, but the sun had broken through the clouds, turning the ocean a shimmery blue-green that seemed better suited to the Bahamas than northern Scotland. It was pretty, though, and for a moment, Nolie tipped her head back, sucking in a deep breath of clean, salty air. Out here, it was easier to pretend they'd just imagined that boy. Things like that didn't really happen, did they?

When she turned to look at Bel, her friend was pale, her expression troubled.

"You aren't going to tell your da about this, are you?" Bel asked, and since Nolie hadn't expected that question, it took her a second to reply.

"*Are* you?" Bel repeated.

Nolie shook her head, confused. "No, I won't. What could I even say?"

Bel tugged the sleeves of her rain slicker over her hands. "I don't know."

They stood there in silence for a second, but then Bel looked down the beach toward the harbor. "My dad and Jaime are back with the boat," she said. "I'd better go see them."

Nolie wasn't sure if Bel really wanted to see her family, or if she just wanted to be alone for a while, so she just nodded. "Okay, cool. See you tomorrow?"

But Bel was already dashing down the beach, leaving Nolie to stare after her.

When Nolie got back to the Institute, her dad was down-stairs in the big room that had probably been used for dining back when this was a regular house. He was sitting at a table, staring at a bunch of computer printouts, and made a little grunt of greeting when Nolie said hello.

She thought about asking when they could go back to the house, but instead, she heaved herself up onto the table near the window, her feet kicking in the empty space. "Dad?"

"Nol?" he said, without looking up from the papers in front of him.

She glanced back out the window. It had turned out to be such a pretty evening after the grossness of the morning. The weather could change quickly like that in Scotland, Nolie was learning.

It was weird, but on sunny days like this, the fog was creepier. On cloudy days, the fog seemed to blend into the sky and water, but with the bright blue sky and the water not looking nearly as hard, the fog stood out even more, and it seemed to roll and seethe like something alive.

Shivering a little, Nolie turned her attention back to her dad. "Before the scientists came, what did the vil-lagers think the fog was?"

That made her dad look up, his eyes blue behind his

glasses. "Oh, all kinds of things," he said, putting his papers on the desk and giving her his full attention. "There are lots of different legends. Like maybe it was the edge of the world past that fog bank and you could just sail right off. Or that it was the blue men of the Minch."

Nolie wrinkled her nose. "Blue men of the Minch?"

Laughing, her dad nodded. "All kinds of magic things in Scotland. The blue men are like . . . mermen, I guess is the closest thing? The Minch is the water between Scotland and the Hebrides islands, so the idea was that they'd lure sailors into the water and wreck their ships, that kind of thing. But there was nothing about fog in those legends, so it never caught hold. And of course there was stuff about witches and curses and ghosts and who knows what." He laughed a little. "That's nothing new, though. Go anywhere in Scotland, and you'll find a dozen stories like that. There's a castle south of here that they say the devil built, and supposedly the loch there has a mermaid."

He smiled and shook his head, but Nolie could tell that even if the scientist in him couldn't believe those kinds of stories, he still liked them.

She did, too, and now she had a pretty big reason to believe them.

"Do you ever think that maybe the legends aren't wrong?" Nolie asked, hopping off the table. The floor creaked under her feet as she moved closer to the window.

This was her favorite spot in the whole house, and she imagined the people who used to live here loved it, too. Killer fog or not, it was a pretty view.

Her dad chuckled again, and she heard the scratch of his pen as he moved back to his work. "Mermen and curses?" he asked. "It sure makes a better story, Nol, I'll give you that. But I'm not really in the business of believing those kinds of things."

Nolie understood that, but she wanted to point out that life was way more fun when you believed in *all* kinds of things.

She said that to her dad now, and he looked up at her again. He'd had a gray streak in his beard for years, but it seemed wider now, and there were deeper lines around his eyes when he smiled at her.

"I agree, Nolie Mae," he said. "But science is fun, too. And hey, years ago, science and magic were basically the same thing."

"But what if there *were* something magic that happened that science couldn't explain?" she went on, still thinking of Albert in that cave. "Like, okay. Those people who have disappeared?"

Her dad was watching her, his elbows resting on his knees, and he nodded, encouraging her to go on.

"What if . . . what if one of them came back?"

Her dad raised his eyebrows and tilted his head down

a little, looking at her over the rims of his glasses. "Well, then we'd just say they hadn't really been lost," he started, and Nolie fought the urge to groan, frustrated.

"No, that's not what I meant. I mean ... let's say someone disappeared a hundred years ago, and then they came *back*, but looked the same as they did the day they left?"

That was getting a little too close to the truth of it, but she was curious to hear what her dad would say.

To her relief, he didn't laugh, or wave her off, or say that was impossible. Instead, he mulled it over, fingers drumming on the arms of his chair as he leaned back.

"If that happened," he finally said, "there would be a lot of research to do. Tests to run. The anti-aging people would be all over it, of course, not to mention every magazine in the world. Every newspaper."

Nolie knew that, but still, the thought of Albert strapped into machines, people running tests on him, his face all over the internet ...

For the first time since she'd seen him walking on the beach, she really wished Bel *had* been right, and that it was only some kind of prank.

Changing the subject, she asked, "So what do the people in the village think *now*?"

"It's hard to tell. I think they like the idea of it staying a mystery, because it helps their tourism industry. People want to come see something they don't understand, and if we work out what it is, they might stop coming."

"Makes sense," Nolie said. "Would people go see Loch Ness if they didn't think there was a big monster in it?"

Dad's chair creaked as he leaned back. "Exactly. The people who've disappeared aren't a mystery. Their boats sank. But that's not as romantic as *vanished without a trace into a strange fog.*"

Nolie turned away from the window. "None of that seems romantic to me." She thought again about all those faces on the back wall of Bel's parents' shop. "It's just sad."

Her dad nodded. "That it is. Which is why it would be nice to figure out what's making the fog. If we got into it, saw what's what, we might be able to recover some of the boats. Give closure to the families who've lost people."

Scooting his chair back up to the table, Dad tapped the papers in front of him with the end of his pen. "It would also be nice to know why it's getting closer."

The words made Nolie blink, and for some reason, she immediately thought of Albert MacLeish, or the boy who claimed to be Albert MacLeish. Albert in the cave, and the little rowboat in the other, bigger cave.

"Closer?" Nolie asked, coming to stand behind her dad as he flipped on the computer. "What do you mean?"

Her dad rubbed a hand over the back of his neck.

"That's what the data says," he told her. "It's nothing all that new—the Boundary fluctuates by a foot or so all the time, but now it's two meters closer to shore, and that happened overnight. We've never registered a change that big before, or that fast."

It couldn't be a coincidence, Albert showing up and the fog moving nearer to shore, could it?

"What will you do?" she asked. "If it comes closer?"

Her dad pushed away from his desk. "Well, not much we can do. It has to be an atmospheric disturbance of some kind, and if I had to guess, I'd say the fog will move back soon enough."

He got up then, walking toward the kitchen and the coffeepot, and Nolie trailed behind, fidgeting with the ends of her scarf. "You don't think the fog could, like . . . eat the village, do you?"

Pouring himself a cup of coffee, Dad glanced over his shoulder at Nolie. "The fog doesn't eat people, kiddo. It's a weather thing, not a monster. I promise."

Hearing him say it like that, so calmly, should've made her feel better, but instead, it just made Nolie feel worse. It was easy for Dad not to think something weird was happening when he didn't know about the hundred-year-old boy who'd just turned up. "What about the lighthouse?" she asked.

When her dad just raised his eyebrows at her, Nolie

96

said, "Bel said there was an island out in the fog, and that it might have a lighthouse on it."

Her dad made a kind of humming sound, picking up his mug and taking a sip. "Well, you've been here all of a day, and already gotten more information out of the locals than we ever have. We found the lighthouse on our readings, but no one would ever confirm that it existed, or when it had been built. We sent one of the drones to take pictures of it just the other day."

Excited, he turned back to his computer and opened a file. A blurry black-and-white shot filled the monitor. "The drone didn't come back," he told her, "but it sent a couple of pictures before it crashed."

"Or got eaten," Nolie corrected, but her dad just smiled, shaking his head.

"The fog *doesn't* eat things, Nol. But look, there's the lighthouse."

He tapped the screen, and Nolie could just make out a tall tower with a white spot at its top. That had to be the light, but the picture was so blurry, it was hard to tell. Then her dad clicked another file, and there was the tower again, a dim gray blob, only this time, no white spot.

She remembered what Bel had said on the beach that first day, about a ghost in the lighthouse. Of course, Bel had *also* said she wasn't sure there even *was* a lighthouse out there, but here it was, in black and white on Dad's computer.

Nolie leaned closer to the screen. "Did the light go out?" she asked, and her dad squinted.

"We're not sure. Can't even tell if that *was* a light, to be honest. The weather conditions made seeing anything pretty tough."

"But this happened just a couple of days ago?" Nolie asked, and her dad nodded.

"Yup. Lot of interesting stuff happening at the Boundary right now."

"Yeah," she muttered, still frowning at the blurry lighthouse. "I'll say."

CHAPTER 10

"YOU'RE SURE YOU WANT TO DO THIS?"

Bel had asked Nolie that at least a dozen times already, it felt like, but looking at her friend's pale face as she clutched the straps on her life jacket, it seemed like she should probably ask again. For a girl who seemed to like all kinds of scary things—ghosts, monsters, really bright wellies—Nolie was clearly a little more cautious when it came to boats.

"'Course," Nolie answered, her voice a lot braver than her face. "Can't come to Journey's End and not go out on the *Bonny Bel*, right?"

"Shuddup," Bel said, elbowing Nolie slightly. Before Bel was born, the boat had been called the *Foghorn*, a joke about the Boundary, but her dad had rechristened it after her. When she was littler, she'd liked that, having a boat named after her. Lately, though, it seemed more embarrassing than anything else.

But Nolie smiled, looking relaxed for the first time

since she'd set foot on the boat. "It's so awesome to have a boat named after you!" she insisted. "If the SS *Nolie Mae* were a thing, I'd tell *everyone*."

"Of course you would," Bel said. She'd only known Nolie for a few days, but she was beginning to understand a lot about how her new friend worked. Nolie had a personality to match all that bright red hair: loud, fun, and definitely a standout.

Even when she was clearly scared.

The boat ride hadn't been their original plan for the day. Nolie had walked down to the shop that morning, and they'd both wanted to search the beach for Al. However, other than the boat—the *Selkie*—there was no sign of him. Not even footprints in the wet sand. And after about an hour of calling for him and searching the cave, they'd come back up to the harbor just in time to see the *Bonny Bel* getting ready for its noon trip. Bel had suggested the ride, thinking Nolie might like to see the Boundary, and also pointing out that they might get a better, wider look at the beach from out on the sea.

Nolie had agreed easily enough, but it had been clear from the second they'd set foot on board that this was not Nolie's idea of fun.

The boat rumbled away from the dock, and Nolie dropped her hands to clutch the railing.

"You promise no one's died on this boat, right?" she asked Bel, but before Bel could reply, her brother Jaime appeared at her side, his dark blond hair wind-ruffled, his cheeks red. He'd put a slicker on over his long-sleeved T-shirt, and he was wearing a pair of hiking boots even though their dad always wanted him to wear wellies. Jaime had always liked to rebel in little ways.

"Not a single dead body on this boat in years," he promised Nolie, then winked. "Well, none we tell the tourists about."

"Jaime," Bel chided, punching her older brother in the arm as Nolie seemed to turn as gray as the sky.

"Teasing," he promised, and then he ruffled Bel's hair like he always did. "So this is Nolie," he said, turning back to smile at her. "Yer da's one of the scientists at the Institute, yeah?"

Nolie nodded, swallowing hard, and Jaime glanced at Bel, eyebrows raised. "You ever been on a boat, Nolie?" he asked, and she shook her head so fast her red hair flew around her face in a blur.

"Nope. I've never been a boat person, I guess. I have a motion sickness thing?" She said it like a question, but there was no doubt she was going from gray to green now. So maybe it was less that Nolie was scared, and more that she was afraid of throwing up. That made sense.

"Ah, no worries, lass," Jaime told her, patting her shoulders. "This ride is as gentle as they come."

Bel knew for a fact that wasn't true, but when Nolie's grip on the rail eased, she was grateful Jaime had said it.

"You gonna come up top for the show, or stay down here?" he asked them.

Bel took one look at Nolie's face and knew there was no way she was getting her up the winding metal stairs that led to the top deck. There were rows of benches up there where people could sit and take pictures of the Boundary. Bel's dad and Jaime took turns either driving the boat or working the microphone, giving the tourists all the facts on it: There were records of it for the past five hundred years, but no mention before that; there were over forty known disappearances in the fog; in 1933, scientists from America had come to study it; and now no boats were allowed any closer than the *Bonny Bel* would be getting.

It was a routine Bel had heard hundreds of times, one she could do in her sleep. One, she thought, that *she* might have to do one day. Simon had done the lecture before he went to uni, and if Jaime decided to go next year, there'd be no one but her until Jack got a lot older.

"We'll stay down here," she told Jaime, and he nodded before heading for the stairs, his boots clanging against the metal.

"So will you give me the tour?" Nolie asked, interested.

Leaning on the rail, Bel peered out at the Boundary as the boat chugged closer. "You probably know most everything he'll say," she told Nolie, jerking her chin up to where they could already hear Jaime greeting people over the mic.

"Then tell me the parts you *don't* tell the tourists," Nolie said.

Bel paused to think about it. "They never mention the wee island that's in the fog. Or the legend that there's a lighthouse on it."

Nolie flexed her hands on the rail. Her knuckles were bright red, and Bel could've kicked herself for forgetting to bring gloves. "There is a lighthouse," she said. "I saw it."

Bel flinched. "What?"

"My dad said they sent a drone into the Boundary last week," Nolie suddenly said, the words coming out in a rush. "It took pictures, and you could see the lighthouse in a few of them. In some it was lit and in others it wasn't. Like it had gone out."

Bel twisted her ring. Maybe that was why Mum had been so against the drones? Because it would mess with the lighthouse?

Had her mum even known the lighthouse existed? If she had, she'd certainly never told Bel. "Do they think they're the ones who put out the light?" Bel asked.

"They have to be, right? It's the only thing that makes sense. Which means . . . Bel, do you think Albert coming back is because my dad accidentally put out the light?"

Bel could only shake her head, trying to get her thoughts in order. The Institute sent drones. The light went out. Suddenly, a boy who should've been dead a hundred years ago was back. All of it had to be connected, but what did it even *mean?* Suddenly she wished they'd spent more time looking for Al that morning, even if he'd been hiding from them.

Nolie was watching her, shivering a little from the wind and the spray kicked up by the *Bonny Bel.* They were getting closer to the Boundary now, the wall of fog rising up from the water, and even though Bel had been seeing it her whole life, had made this same boat trip more times than she could count, it still made her heart seem to rise up in her chest, and she could feel the hair on the back of her neck stand up.

And as she looked at the fog, she thought of meeting Al yesterday in the cave.

Next to her, Nolie took a deep breath, both hands on the railing now, but even though she was still a little pale, she was leaning forward, the salt spray and damp making her bright hair curl around her face.

"Hooooooly cow," she murmured, and Bel smiled, oddly pleased. If Nolie had hated this whole trip, it would've "bummed" her out, too, seeing as how it was her idea. And her boat. (That's how Nolie would've said it, anyway; Bel made a note to remind her that "bum" meant something really different in Scotland.)

But Nolie turned to Bel with wide eyes, a grin splitting her face. "This is so totally magic," she said, and Bel grinned back.

"You think so?"

"'Meteorological phenomena,'" Nolie said, shaking her head. "Try 'Super Crazy Magic Fog Probably Made By Witches.'"

"I'm starting to think you might be right," Bel agreed. "Oh, and you know, now that you're in Scotland, you should probably say 'holy hairy coo' instead of 'holy cow.' To fit in."

Nolie screwed up her face. "Why do I have the feeling you're making that up?" she asked, and Bel smiled. She would have nudged Nolie with her elbow, but her friend was still clutching the railing pretty hard, and Bel didn't want to scare her.

They were as close to the fog as the boat ever went, now. It loomed up over them, reaching into the sky and blending with the clouds, although Bel could always tell where the fog ended and the clouds began. The fog tended to look more solid, for one thing, but there was also the way it moved, like it was churning. Somewhere in there was a rocky island and the lighthouse, and if Nolie was right, it had gone dark.

The light going out was a weirdly sad thought.

Upstairs, Jaime was still talking, but Bel couldn't make out the words over the sound of the engines. The boat was turning now, putting the Boundary behind them, and Bel frowned, glancing at her watch. The tour lasted exactly forty-five minutes. Fifteen to get out to the Boundary, fifteen to let people take pictures, and then fifteen minutes back to the docks. But according to the green plastic watch on her wrist, the trip had taken just a couple of minutes less than normal. Had Jaime cut picture-taking time? Or had they reached the Boundary faster than usual?

The ride back to the docks was smooth enough, and Nolie had returned to a pretty normal color, although Bel saw that she kept glancing over a shoulder to look back at the Boundary. It wasn't until they were nearly at the docks that Nolie said, "Since this is apparently a confessional boat ride, I should probably tell you . . . it's more than just the light going out. My dad says it's getting closer. The Boundary."

Startled, Bel looked at her friend. "What?"

Nolie waved one hand. "Science stuff. Just said that it's moved a little bit closer, but that it does that sometimes? Although he said this time it was kind of a lot."

Docking the boat never took long—Dad and Jaime

always said that the sooner you get everyone off the boat after seeing the Boundary, the sooner you could get them into the gift shop—and it was only a few minutes before Nolie and Bel were lined up to step back onto the dock, Nolie shucking off her life jacket with a look of immense relief.

"Okay, so yay Magic Fog," she said, hanging the jacket on a peg with the rest of them, "but still never going to be a fan of boats."

"Fair enough," Bel replied, reaching into her pocket for a hair elastic. "Do you want to go back down to the beach?" she started, while tying up her hair—then came up short as they stepped onto the dock. "Whoa."

"What?" Nolie asked, and Bel nodded toward the figure standing at the far end of the harbor.

"It's Maggie," she said. "Mrs. McLeod. The lady who lives in that big house on the hill."

Nolie peered around Bel, and then her shoulder sagged a little. "Oh man, she doesn't look like a creepy old witch lady at *all*. She's wearing *jeans*."

Now that they were back on solid ground, Bel felt safe about nudging Nolie. "She's not a creepy old witch lady; she's just old," she reminded her.

Mum had told Bel that Maggie had all her groceries delivered, and that she came down the hill once a year for a doctor appointment, but Bel had only caught a glimpse of her once, maybe. So it was odd seeing her standing there in her jumper and jeans, white hair pulled back into a tight bun. She was looking out at the Boundary, her lips clamped tight together, arms crossed.

Bel looked in the same direction, wondering what Maggie was thinking about.

"Her clothes aren't spooky," Nolie said in a low voice, "but she kind of is? A little bit, at least?"

Bel was about to agree when she noticed her mum walking across to the boat, almost running. "Hi, sweetie," she said to Bel, clearly distracted, and then she was heading onto the boat toward Bel's dad.

Bel watched her parents talking, and saw her dad put his hands on his hips, chin tilted down as he listened to Mum. Jaime was with them, too, his sandy eyebrows lifting at whatever it was Mum was saying.

Bel didn't want to interrupt, so she waited until Jaime was off the boat to corner him.

"What's going on?" she asked, and Jaime looked between her and Nolie before scrubbing a hand over his hair.

"Something's amiss, seems like," he told them. "With the Boundary."

And then he nodded at Nolie. "Your da's gone and called a meeting."

CHAPTER 11

THE INSTITUTE DIDN'T HAVE A CONFERENCE ROOM, so they'd filled the old ballroom with as many folding chairs as they could find. It still hadn't been enough, though; Nolie was standing up near the back with dozens of other people. The whole village of Journey's End had turned out tonight, and Nolie wasn't sure if it was the press of people or their expressions—it was like a deep V was carved just over the bridge of every nose—that made her sort of wish she'd stayed home with a book and Sir Woolington.

Up at the front of the room, Nolie's dad stood on an overturned crate of some kind, a sheaf of index cards in his hands. His eyes scanned the crowd and the cards in his hands shook. Outside, it was raining again, and water ran in streams down the windows behind him. Even through all the rain, though, Nolie could see the Boundary, undulating way out at sea.

For the first time, Nolie wondered if her dad had

chosen this room not because it was the biggest one, but so that he would have the Boundary behind him for people to look at.

Making herself as small as she could, Nolie huddled against the paneled wall, thinking that she might just try to sneak away and hide out in Dad's office until this was all over. But before she could make a break for it, someone was nudging her side.

Bel.

She wasn't alone, either. There was a little boy, maybe five, holding her hand, his hair a few shades lighter than Bel's own dark blond, but they had the same nose and hazel eyes. He was dragging his heels a little bit, and Nolie saw Bel gently pull him forward.

"This is my brother Jack," she said. "I'm meant to be watching him."

Nolie didn't really know how to talk to little kids, so she just gave Jack a wave. "Hi."

He studied her with solemn eyes before turning to Bel. "Can I have a lolly now?"

Bel tugged him a bit closer. "If you're good and quiet during the meeting, then you can."

Jack looked like he might argue, but then Bel glanced back to Nolie. "This is a bit mad, isn't it?" she asked breathlessly, and Nolie nodded.

"It's a lot mad." She knew that Bel meant *mad* like crazy, not angry, but it was that, too. There was a humming in the air like a swarm of bees, and the whole room felt too hot and too crowded.

But now that Bel was here, Nolie didn't feel like running away as much.

"What will they do?" she asked, lowering her head close to Bel's. "If the fog comes closer?"

"It won't," Bel said firmly. She nodded her head, and hair fell from behind one ear, brushing against her chin.

Jack had sat down at their feet now and was pulling at his shoelaces, clearly ignoring whatever his sister was talking about.

Frowning, Nolie fiddled with her sleeve. "But you said there were stories—"

"Aye, stories." Raising up on her tiptoes, Bel surveyed the room. "Legends, that's all. If the Boundary had ever moved closer, we'd know it."

Nolie's dad was still looking over his notes and didn't seem in that big of a hurry to talk, so Nolie said, "But Dad's instruments. The readings."

Bel shrugged. "Sometimes science is wrong."

Nolie didn't think that was a very good answer. "What about Albert?" she whispered, and Bel looked over at her, brow furrowed.

"Who's Albert?" Jack asked, looking up at the two of them, and rather than answer, Bel fished into her pocket for a sucker, which she quickly handed off to him.

He took it with a smile, noisily tearing the paper off, all thoughts of Albert forgotten.

Nolie would've used the distraction to talk to Bel some more, but then her dad was gesturing for the room to quiet down, so she didn't get a chance to say anything else.

"I'd like to thank everyone for coming tonight," her dad started, but that's as far as he got before Bel's brother Jaime, sitting in the front row, called out.

"Not like we had much choice!"

Nolie's stomach twisted, her face feeling hot as she watched her dad fumble through his cards again. "I realize the announcement was a little abrupt, but we thought the sooner we talked to everyone about this, the better off we'll all be."

Her dad said *we*, but there was no one else from the Institute here tonight except for his assistant, Alan, standing behind him and trying to look serious with his clipboard. Her dad's face was nearly as red as Nolie's hair, and Nolie thought he looked as nervous as she felt.

"There shouldn't be cause for alarm—yet—but according to our recent observations, the Boundary is moving closer to shore."

Nolie's dad wasn't speaking loudly, but she felt his words land like little bombs all around the room. A buzz of whispers and murmurs started up, and Nolie kept her eyes trained on her dad's face, waiting for him to say more. He was smiling a bit, but she was pretty sure it was the same nervous smile she gave when presenting in front of the class. And usually her classmates weren't watching her the same way these people were watching her dad now, shoulders stiff, expressions closed.

"It—it could move back," her dad added, "and almost certainly will, but if it keeps moving forward at the rate it is right now, that . . . that will be of concern," he finished, clearing his throat and shuffling his index cards.

There was a flush still staining his neck, and Nolie saw him lift his eyes to the crowd again, then wince slightly as he looked back down at the cards.

Whatever he was about to say, he didn't want to say it.

"With that in mind, though, for the time being, it seems like it would be in all our best interests if tour boats to the Boundary ceased operation."

Next to Nolie, Bel drew in a sharp breath, and Nolie saw Bel's dad stand up in the front row.

"So you want us to stop *working* until your type figure out what's the trouble?" His voice was deep and husky, his accent a little thicker than Bel's. At her feet, Jack looked up, and Nolie watched her dad frown.

"I understand that's an inconvenience—" Nolie's dad started, but Bel's dad just laughed.

"An *inconvenience*? It'll be a lot more than that if we're out of work for long."

A woman a few rows behind Bel's dad stood up. She was older, her dark hair streaked with gray, a red scarf around her throat. "Kenneth's right," she said. "And if the tour boats can't go out, the tourists will stop coming. This town doesn't survive without them eating in our cafés, buying our petrol, buying all those"—she waved a hand toward Bel's parents—"knickknacks and what have you. You're asking us to shut down our lives because of a wee bit of fog? This is *our* town, and there's *always* been fog."

Another voice piped up from somewhere in the row of chairs. "The people of Journey's End know best what do to about the Boundary. All the Institute does is stare at it and type things into a computer."

There were more murmurs of agreement, and Nolie felt her face go even hotter. This wasn't going well at all, and she could see her dad clutching his cards tighter.

"This is for everyone's safety," he reminded them. "And may come to nothing."

"*We'll* come to nothing if you have your way," Bel's dad said, and Nolie glanced over at Bel. The corners of her mouth were turned down, and she kept tugging at the sleeves of her sweater, pulling them over her fingers.

She wouldn't look at Nolie.

"I can't make you stop the boats," Nolie's dad said, and although his face was just as red, his voice was firm. Nolie had never seen her dad angry before—he had never been around enough to get angry with her—but she thought he might be now. "I'm asking you to, though. Just to be on the safe side."

"And I'm telling you we won't," Bel's mum answered, rising to her feet. She pointed a finger toward the window behind Nolie's dad. "If the Boundary is a problem, *we'll* handle it."

Nolie's dad may have called the meeting, but it was Bel's mum who ended it. With that, she turned and gestured to her husband, who got up, signaling for Bel to follow. Jaime rose to his feet, too, and soon everyone was standing and heading for the door.

Nolie looked up at her dad, her heart in her throat, and while he was clearly not happy, he didn't say anything to stop the crowd from leaving.

"Bel—" Nolie said, turning to the other girl.

But Bel was already scooping up Jack and walking toward her family, disappearing into the crowd.

CHAPTER 12

"WELL, THAT WAS A RIGHT DOG'S DINNER," BEL'S DAD said as he unlocked the front door. Bel, her mum, Jaime, and Jack all trundled in after him, stamping their feet on the mat first.

"It won't come to anything," Mum insisted, taking off her jacket. "Come to think of it, business will probably pick up."

Jaime was already at the counter, turning on the electric kettle, and Bel's dad braced both hands on the back of a kitchen chair, looking at her mum with raised eyebrows. "How d'you reckon?"

"The scarier the Boundary is, the more people will want to see it," Jaime answered, glancing over his shoulder, and even though Bel's mum rolled her eyes, she smiled all the same.

"Well, I was going to say it will make the place seem more mysterious, but yes, that, too."

Bel's dad didn't seem as convinced, shaking his head as

he sat in his chair and scooped Jack onto his lap, studying the sticky blue lolly ring around Jack's mouth. "The Institute has been looking for an excuse to shut down the boat trips for years now, Fee," he said to Mum. "If they can prove it's dangerous . . ."

"It is dangerous," Jack said, reaching for a stack of paper napkins on the table. Bel had to move fast to get them out of his reach, knowing he'd only tear them up. Her little brother scowled, then added, "It eats people, don't it?"

"Doesn't it," Bel's whole family corrected in unison, and then Bel's dad tickled Jack's ribs, sending him into fits of laughter.

"The fog won't eat you, Jackie," Dad said, blowing a raspberry on Jack's neck, "because *I'm* going to eat you first!"

Jack kept shrieking and giggling, and even though Bel's mum said something about not riling him up this close to bedtime, her dad didn't let up.

"Off to bed!" Bel called, and Jaime gave her a nod even as Jack yelled, "Noooooo, Bel, save me!"

"It's too late for that now!" Dad said in the same growly voice he'd used for all of them when they played this game, and Jack dissolved into another fit of laughter.

"'Night, sweetheart," Mum said, catching Bel by the door and pressing a quick kiss to the crown of her head. But when Bel went to walk away, her mum caught her arm gently, keeping her from leaving. "You're sure you're all right?" she asked. "I know you're good friends with Dr. Stanhope's daughter. Tonight didn't . . . mess that up?"

Bel shook her head, even though she hadn't gotten the chance to talk to Nolie. But then, Nolie didn't seem like the type to get mad at her over something like this.

Or at least she hoped she wasn't. After everything with Leslie, Bel wasn't sure she really got how friends worked anymore.

Bel leaned against the wall and looked at her mum. "Did you know there was a lighthouse out there? In the fog?"

Mum pushed her hair back from her eyes, sighing. "Well, I'd never seen it," she said with a shrug. "No one had, but it doesn't surprise me. This used to be a fishing village, after all, and a lighthouse certainly would've been handy around this coast."

Bel nodded, but wished she could explain to Mum why it bothered her that she'd been wrong about the lighthouse—that she'd never even *asked* before. What else might she be wrong about?

As she made her way up to her little room under the eaves, Bel wondered again if she and Nolie should've said something tonight. But would anyone have listened? And it wasn't like they had Al *there* to prove what they were saying anyway. What if everyone had just thought they were mental?

What if they *were* mental?

Bel was still frowning when she opened her bedroom door, so lost in her thoughts that it took her a second to register that she wasn't alone.

There was someone sitting on her bed, and as Bel's heart thudded hard in her chest, Al stood awkwardly, raising one hand in a kind of wave. "Hullo."

Nolie could tell her dad was frustrated when they got home. He did the same thing Nolie did, putting things down just a little too hard, flopping into his chair instead of sitting in it, and Nolie followed behind, perching on the edge of the couch.

"You really think they won't stop the boat trips?" she asked, and he gave a sigh, scrubbing his hair back with one hand.

"I think this village can be stubborn," he said. "And I don't just mean the people in it. This is a place that sometimes feels like it shouldn't exist, but here it is. Here it stays. And that's the thing. They've stayed so long now that none of this worries them. All these stories of the fog coming close before . . ." Another sigh, and this time he tipped back his head, looking at the ceiling, tapping his fingers on the arm of the chair. "The thing is, no one can remember what happened then. It's all just legends and stories passed down, and trying to suss out the facts is just about impossible."

Nolie got the feeling her dad wasn't really talking to her; she just happened to be in the room. That was okay, though. She did the same thing to her mom, always needing to hear a problem out loud before she could figure out how to solve it. There were times she even talked it out alone in her bedroom, something that always embarrassed her if she thought about other people knowing.

And sure enough, her dad kept looking at the ceiling as he talked. "If the fog did keep moving inland, there's no way of knowing what would happen. Like I said, the boats that disappear into it, they just sink. It can't be . . . *absorbing* them, or whatever the local stories stay. That's just stuff to sell books and T-shirts and those stuffed lambs."

"Who also wear T-shirts," Nolie reminded her dad. "That say *Stand baaaaack.*"

Her dad laughed at that, shaking his head a little. "That is clever, I have to admit," he said.

"I've named mine Sir Woolington," Nolie told him. "So that when he goes back to Georgia, he can lord his status over my other stuffed animals."

That made her dad smile, but it was a sad kind of smile, one that wobbled just a little bit.

"And the next time you come here, you probably won't even like stuffed animals anymore," he said.

She wasn't all that attached to them now, really, but Nolie didn't want to say that in case it hurt his feelings.

Then Dad sighed, rubbing a hand over the back of his neck. "I hate that this is happening while you're here," he said. "I feel like I've been at work the whole time, and you must be bored." He gave a little snort, shaking his head. "Bring you over here to spend time with you, and then let you run wild around the village instead."

"I like running wild," Nolie told him quickly. "Making friends, having fun new international experiences . . ."

She was only kind of joking. The truth was, it had been really nice spending these first few days with Bel, not only because of everything that was happening, but because it meant there hadn't been much time for her to talk with her dad. And since Nolie was afraid he might want to talk about the divorce, she was okay with the not-talking for now.

Nodding, Nolie's dad gave her knee another pat before shifting back. "Okay. Well. Good, then. I'm glad you've made a friend. And don't let this meeting tonight worry you about that. You and Bel should be just fine," he told her. "The last thing the Institute wants to do is shut down anyone's livelihoods; we just want everyone to stay informed."

Nolie didn't bother mentioning that the meeting tonight hadn't seemed like informing so much as warning, and she could understand why that made Bel's parents angry. "It's their home, though," she said to her dad. "So I guess they feel like they know what's best."

Her dad swung around in his chair, turning his computer on. "And they do, in a lot of ways," he said. "It's just that we know some things, too."

You don't, Nolie thought, and she came way too close to saying it out loud. Her dad *didn't* know about Albert, but that was because she hadn't told him, and even if she had, would he believe her? What was more likely, that there was some kid playing a prank, or that a one-hundred-and-something-year-old guy had come back from the Boundary?

"I'm going on up to bed," she said now, giving her dad a light punch on the shoulder. "Let me know if we all get eaten by fog in the night."

Either her dad didn't really hear her, or he was getting used to her joking, because he just lifted a hand and said, "Will do," his gaze still trained on the screen in front of him.

Shaking her head, Nolie made her way down the hall to her little bedroom that looked over the back garden.

It still wasn't dark yet, looking more like late afternoon than evening. Still enough light that she didn't bother turning on her lamp as she opened the wardrobe across from her bed. This house was nice, and Nolie liked the airiness of her room, the white walls, the deep green duvet cover on her bed, but it was still really different from her house in Georgia. None of the bedrooms had closets, for one thing, and the rooms all felt smaller than she was used to.

Her jacket was hanging from a hook just inside the wardrobe door, and she reached into the pocket, pulling out the letter her mom had sent.

Smiling, she sat down on her bed and opened it.

It wasn't actually a letter, but a card, and Nolie wrinkled her nose when she saw the five guys on it, all wearing white tank tops and black pants, two with backward baseball caps. When she opened it, a song started up, something cheesy about girls not needing makeup, and she giggled even as the sight of her mom's handwriting made her eyes sting.

Nolie Mae, she'd written, *I know you love boy bands, so I had to get this card just for you. ;)*

"I hate boy bands," Nolie murmured, but she was smiling even as she rubbed her nose. *I miss you sooooo much, and hope you're having a wonderful time! The house is quiet without my sweet girl stomping around and making me laugh. I've started talking to Fred the Goldfish without you here, and I have to say, he's not nearly as much fun as you. Be good, be sweet, and try to pick up a Scottish accent for me, okay? Love you the most.*

—Mom

P.S. Tell your dad I said hi, and I hope he's picking up an accent, too. Scottish accents for all!

Throat tight, Nolie put the card down on her bed, thinking again that her mom was great, and her *dad* was great, so why couldn't they just . . . be great together? They'd always been the *best* team, the three of them against the world, and Nolie missed that.

A lot.

Sniffling, Nolie went to the window. She was just about to pull down her shade when a face popped up against the glass.

Nolie stumbled backward, stifling a shriek as Bel grinned. The sun made her hair glow around her face.

"What are you doing?" Nolie mouthed, and Bel just waved one hand, clearly signaling for Nolie to follow her. Casting a glance behind her, Nolie thought of her dad, still plugged into his computer, his mind a million miles away.

And after a pause, she opened the window and crawled out.

CHAPTER 13

IT WAS FAIRLY QUIET IN THE VILLAGE AT NIGHT, AND BEL didn't know if that was because the weather had been so poor, or if after the meeting, everyone was doing the same thing that her family had wanted to do—go home and talk it all over. The arcade was closed earlier than normal, and while Bel saw a few people down by the harbor, sipping from Styrofoam cups of tea, on the whole, it was nearly empty.

Which was a good thing, since Nolie was singing a little song under her breath.

"We're sneaking ouuuuut," she whisper-sang. "Sneeeaaaak-iiiiing *ouuuuttt*."

"Shhh!" Bel shushed, even as she smiled, the two of them skirting around the harbor. "The 'sneaking' is the important bit, you nutter."

Nolie gave an easy shrug, kicking a stray rock out of her way. "This moment needed to be commemorated in song," she said, and then she looked over at Bel. Her smile was almost shy.

"And since we're sneaking out and sharing secrets and stuff, I guess that means you're not mad at me."

Bel didn't have time to stop—the sooner they were back, the better—but she did slow down a little. "I thought you might be mad at me, too," she confessed. "Or . . . not *angry*, I s'pose, just . . . it was . . ."

"Super awkward?" Nolie supplied, and Bel gave a tight nod.

They were moving up from the harbor, climbing a slight rise, and Nolie pointed to a little stone plinth that overlooked the water. "What's that?" she asked, and Bel glanced over her shoulder at it.

"Hmm? Oh, just a wee plaque someone put there years ago. It's odd. Just says *In Hope of Forgiveness*, but no names, no dates or anything. Always figured a sailor upset his girlfriend or summat," Bel said, and Nolie frowned in the direction of the plaque, but nodded all the same.

They moved off the pavement and behind the village center. Bel wanted to cut across the field rather than walk up the road to her house so that she could go through the back door.

They were closer to her house now, and she glanced over at Nolie to see if she was looking at it. It wasn't anything as nice as the house that the Institute used, or as pretty as the newer houses by the harbor, like the one Alice's family had bought.

But if Nolie wasn't impressed by Bel's house, she didn't say anything, quietly slipping through the back gate behind Bel, then tiptoeing through the back door.

To Bel's immense relief, Al was still sitting quietly in her room when she sneaked back in, his spine rigid, his hands on his knees. He looked like he was afraid to touch anything, or even move, for fear that he'd make a noise that might lead to his discovery.

"Holy—" Nolie started, and Bel cut her off with a finger pressed against her own lips.

"Shhhhh!" she hissed. "We don't want my parents coming up here. I'm not allowed to have boys in my room."

"Even boys who are technically dead?" Nolie said, and Al shot her that cross look again.

"Not dead," he said stiffly, and Nolie nodded, coming to sit down in Bel's desk chair. "Right, I just mean that you're not the same as a random boy from school. Magical boys who appear out of deadly fog should get a pass, is all I'm saying."

Al's frown deepened, and Bel waved a hand at both of them. "Nolie, he doesn't understand anything you just said, I'd wager, and you'll only upset him. Now both of you, hush, and I'll be right back."

She dashed into the hall, then crept as quietly as she could downstairs, hoping Jaime was still in the kitchen with her family. She could hear the telly on in the living room, and the running water in the bathroom that told her Mum was giving Jack his bath. She'd have to move fast to make sure no one saw her, but she could do that.

Jaime was the only person who used this bedroom now, but he used to share it with Simon, and a lot of Simon's things were still in there. Bel knew Jaime might notice missing clothes, so she was hoping to find an old shirt and trousers that Simon had left behind.

Sure enough, there in the footlocker that Jaime had shoved under the window, Bel unearthed what she was looking for, then tiptoed back upstairs.

Al was in the exact same position that she'd left him in, and Nolie was standing a little closer. "Anyway," she was saying as Bel walked in, "you'll have to work some of that out on your own, but that's my list of the top-five things of the twenty-first century. So far, I mean. We still have a long time to go."

Al stared at her before saying, "What *is* a . . . Netflick?"

"Netflix," Nolie corrected. "And it's the *best*. You just—"

"Clothes!" Bel interrupted, lifting her pilfered bundle, and Al gave a little nod, clearly relieved. She'd grabbed a pair of sweatpants and an old jersey. He could deal with whatever went . . . under them himself.

Her face bright red, Bel handed the clothes to Albert, who took them with shaking hands.

"I can get you some food in a bit if you're hungry," she offered, and Al's head shot up at that, dark eyes bright. He must have been *really* hungry. What did hundred-year-old boys eat?

"So what exactly is going on here?" Nolie asked in a low whisper. "The last time we saw Al, he was threatening to bash our brains out, and now he's just hanging out in your room?"

Al wrung his hands. "I was hiding outside the meeting tonight and heard what's happening. I think you might need my help."

His accent was still thicker than Bel was used to hearing, and she got the sense that Nolie was only catching every other word, if her blinking was anything to go by.

Al shook out the jersey Bel had handed him, studying it. "What is this?"

"It's a shirt," Bel told him, and he gave it a look.

"There are no buttons. It looks like a dress, or a tunic you wrap a babe in."

"We're not giving you baby clothes, promise," Nolie said, but Al only raised his eyebrows at that.

It was weird, Bel thought, seeing his face so expressive. She was used to him staring seriously out of his photograph at the shop, frozen. He'd looked older in the picture, too, but maybe that was just the clothes. She studied him now. Same dark eyes, same long nose and ears that were just a bit too big. A face she'd seen since forever, but not one she'd ever thought she'd see in *person*.

But even though he looked just like Al, *said* he was Al, could he actually *be* Al? He had to be, but at the same time, *how?*

"What's wrong with the clothes I have?" he asked, and Nolie nodded at him, taking in his white shirt and dark pants.

"We don't dress that fancy now. You look like you're going to church. And, like, a weird one where they don't believe in using zippers. No, trust me, you'll like what Bel brought you more."

Al's brows drew together as he studied the clothes, like he wasn't so sure about all of that.

"Can we keep him?" Nolie asked. She had one ankle crossed over the other, and was chewing on her thumbnail, staring at Albert like he might vanish in a puff of smoke at any minute.

"He isn't a puppy," Bel said, nudging Nolie in the ribs as she went to stand next to her.

"I know that," Nolie said. "But . . . Bel, this is *huge*. Maybe it's not about *keeping* him, but *hiding* him."

Albert still sat on the edge of Bel's bed, his face pale and serious.

"Hiding me from what?"

"You've been gone a hundred years, Al," Bel said as she glanced again toward the door. "People are bound to be curious. And curious people can be—"

"Dangerous," Nolie said, her arms crossed tightly over her chest. Her bright red hair was still pulled back in a braid, but lots of it had come loose after the walk from her house.

"Scared," Bel corrected. "People do right stupid things when they're scared, though, so it's just best if we hide you for a bit."

Albert nodded slowly, taking that in. Then he lifted his face to Bel. "Why did you call me 'Al'?"

Bel blinked. Had she done that? Well, that wasn't surprising, seeing as how she'd been calling him Al since she was a wee girl, but it was a bit embarrassing to actually say it to his face.

"It's just what I used to call your picture," she mumbled to Albert now, rolling her shoulders. "Thought you looked like an 'Al.'"

"Al," he repeated, as though trying out the name. And then a smile spread across his face. "People always called me Bertie, and I hated it."

"You were right to hate it," Nolie piped up from the door. "Bertie sounds like someone who has a TV show with puppets."

The smile faded from Albert's face. "I . . . didna understand any of that."

"Don't worry," Bel said. "We can teach you all about the twenty-first century, and TV, and—ooh, and the internet! That'll be fun."

But Al looked dubious, and Bel didn't think she was doing a very good job of convincing him that this wasn't actually terrifying. She wondered then how she would feel, coming back to Journey's End a hundred years from now. What would it be like? Would they have things like flying cars, and if they did, would that seem as weird to her as the TV and cell phones would to Al?

Never mind, they could worry about that later. The internet didn't work very well out here anyway.

"For now," Nolie said, "we can find a place here to hide you for the night. Or maybe at my dad's house? It's big, and—"

"I canna stay with either of you," Al said, his face turning a dull red. "Wouldn't be proper."

Nolie and Bel just stared at him for a second before Nolie said, "Oh, wow. He really *is* a hundred years old, isn't he?"

"Technically, he's one hundred and eleven," Bel said. This really was Albert MacLeish, last seen in 1918, and he was sitting in her bedroom, too scandalized to spend the night at either of their houses.

"So you want to go back to the caves tonight?" Nolie said, sitting back down in Bel's chair. It creaked slightly under her, and even that little noise had Bel looking to the door anxiously, hoping her parents hadn't heard.

"Aye," Al said. He still had Simon's old clothes across his legs, and Bel guessed he was waiting to change until he went back to the caves, and she was grateful for that at least. Bad enough to have a *boy* in her room, even a dead, magical one. A boy changing in her room? Her parents might never let her outside again.

Nolie looked over at Bel. "The Institute, maybe? That place is massive, and no one ever goes to the attic."

Bel looked over to Al, but before he could answer, there was a knock at the door.

"Bel?" her mum called, and then all three of them watched in horror as the doorknob began to turn.

CHAPTER 14

NOLIE HAD WATCHED ENOUGH TV AND READ ENOUGH books to know that hiding boys in closets was bound to happen sooner or later. It was just a part of every girl's life, and honestly, she'd kind of been looking forward to it. Hiding boys, and then having to say things like "This isn't what it looks like!"

That had seemed like a good time.

But she hadn't planned on doing it quite this soon, and she'd definitely never thought she'd be pushing a boy who was over a hundred years old into an overcrowded wardrobe in the corner of a tiny bedroom in Scotland.

Thankfully, Bel had locked the door with a little hook-and-eye closure when she'd come back with those clothes, which gave them enough time to hustle Albert into the closet and out of sight.

"Love, you know I don't like you locking this door!" Bel's mum called, and Nolie closed the wardrobe in Albert's scowling face before giving Bel a thumbs-up, hoping that meant the same thing in Scotland as it did in America.

Bel nodded and went to her door, unlocking it.

Hiding Albert was one thing, but Nolie knew there'd be no space for her, so she figured they'd just hope for the best on that one.

When the door opened to reveal Bel's mum standing there, she didn't even look all that surprised to see Nolie.

"Does your da know you're here?" she asked, and Nolie didn't have to fake a guilty expression. Hiding boys *and* sneaking out. She was really breaking all *kinds* of rules tonight.

But hey, a dead kid had come back to life, which was apparently a *thing that happened here*, so it seemed like rule breaking had been called for.

"No, ma'am," she answered, trying to make her expression as serious as she could. "But Bel and I wanted to talk after everything that happened tonight."

She hoped that threw some guilt on Mrs. McKissick, too, as though the argument between Bel's parents and her dad had really gotten to her and Bel. And it had, a little bit. Until Albert MacLeish showed up again.

Bel's mum sighed, moving her gaze back and forth between the girls. "Okay, but just for a bit," she said. "Then I'll drive you home, all right, Nolie?"

"Yes, ma'am," Nolie said quickly, and Bel's mom gave them both a final once-over with her eyes, then stepped out of the room and shut the door.

Nolie turned back to Bel. "Is this a bad time to say that I really like your room?"

Bel rolled her eyes, but Nolie was telling the truth. This cozy, dim space up high in the McKissick house seemed like the perfect bedroom to her. She was already itching to check out Bel's overstuffed bookcase.

But for now, there was a much more pressing matter.

Nolie stepped over to the wardrobe and opened the door, pressing a finger to her lips to remind Albert to be quiet.

He crept out and sat on the edge of Bel's bed, his bare feet pale against the hardwood floor. Shoes. That was another thing they'd need to work out.

"Okay, we're going to use whispery voices," Nolie told him, demonstrating just how quiet she wanted him to be, "and you're going to tell us what you meant about wanting to help."

"The light—"

"SHHH!" Nolie and Bel hissed in unison, and Albert frowned again. He did have a very stern look, but maybe it wasn't that he was stern so much as that it was weird to see a boy wearing such fancy clothes.

"The light in the lighthouse," Albert continued, finally

keeping his voice low enough. "It must have gone out again. That's why the Boundary is moving closer."

Nolie blinked, taking that in. "I was okay with you being a ghost or maybe a zombie, and I was *way* here for killer fog, but the magic lighthouse keeping the fog back?" she asked. "That seriously sounds like a fairy tale."

Another frown. This kid's face was going to stick that way if he wasn't careful.

Bel sat down on the floor near the bed, folding her legs underneath her. "Maybe start at the beginning," she suggested. "Where have you been since 1918? How did you get here? Why were you—"

Albert held up his hand, then moved it to his head, rubbing at his temple.

"Give him a sec, Bel," Nolie encouraged. "Coming back from the dead is probably really stressful."

Albert's dark eyes met hers. "I was *not* dead," he told her stiffly. "The Boundary had been moving closer. Close enough that it was taking boats from the harbor, and getting too close to the village. Everyone was scared. There had always been a story about the lighthouse—that so long as it was lit, the fog stayed where it was. The town asked for volunteers to go light it. The volunteers never came back."

"Your brother," Bel said softly, and Nolie turned her head, surprised.

"He has a brother?"

"Had," Albert replied. "Edward. He volunteered, but never came back, and the fog kept getting closer. So I decided to do it. Go out there myself. I couldn't even tell you why, really." Pausing, he rubbed the back of his neck, looking at the floor. "I'd found a wee rowboat on the beach one day, and it just seemed ..."

Albert looked up, fixing Nolie and Bel with his dark eyes. "It seemed as though I were meant to take it. And it *worked*. I lit the light, but when I tried to row out, the fog was too thick. I kept rowing, though, and then the fog finally thinned out. And then I rowed to shore."

He started rubbing his temples again.

"To shore, and right into the twenty-first century," Nolie finished, shaking her head. "How long did you think you were rowing?"

Albert shook his head, too. "Felt like forever and only a few minutes all at once. The fog does tricky things to your mind."

Bel had pulled her knees up to her chest now, arms wrapped tight around them.

"It was ... strange," he said. "When the fog broke and I got closer to shore, the boats in the harbor were different, and louder, and ..." He shook his head. "And then I met the two of you."

He said it all so easily, like he was describing any regular day. But he'd come back to a world that was missing everyone he'd loved, everyone he'd cared about. Didn't he feel that? Or did people from his time do a better job holding in their feelings?

It had started to rain outside, the sound soft against the roof and windows, and Nolie huddled a little deeper into her hoodie.

"What happened last time?" she asked. "When the fog came into the village?"

Al was looking at the jersey in his lap, but he lifted his head at that, lips pressed tightly together. "It *took* things," he said slowly.

Nolie felt goose bumps prickle her arms and legs. Maybe it was because they were sitting in a dim room on a rainy night with a boy who might not be a ghost, but was definitely *something* weird.

"What kinds of things?" she asked, imagining the fog sliding into people's pockets, stealing whatever it was people carried in pockets in 1918. Pipes? Watches?

"Houses," Albert replied. "People. Anything it touched vanished, just like the boats."

"Oh," Nolie said, sitting back in the chair. "That's . . . pretty serious."

From her spot on the floor, Bel asked, "So the light

went out, the fog came in. You went and lit the light, and the fog must have rolled back to the lighthouse, but *you* were still stuck in it."

Albert nodded.

Bel sat up a little straighter. "All right, so as long as the light is lit, the fog doesn't come closer?"

"Seems that way," Albert said.

Bel thought that over, her fingers playing with the fringe at the edge of the little floor rug underneath her. "Which means someone must have lit it *before*, right? And maybe gotten stuck rowing around in the fog like you did?"

"Nice one," Nolie said, stretching out her leg to nudge Bel's arm with the toe of her sneaker. "You're probably really good at word problems in math."

Bel waved her off, but she was smiling a little, and Nolie looked back to Albert, waiting for his answer.

"I think there had been," he said at last. "But it wasn't a proper story. Just whispers. There was a bit of strangeness, though. When the fog moved closer, the village called a meeting. My brother and I weren't allowed to go, but ..."

"You sneaked," Nolie supplied. "Which is legit." She pointed at herself and Bel. "We totally sneaked tonight."

Al paused, but then gave a little nod and continued. "Yes, we ... sneaked. And there was a girl in that meeting, a girl I'd never seen before. One of the men, our neighbor, Mr. MacMillan—he asked her why she'd come back."

"So maybe she lit the light, then came back when it went out, just like you," Nolie said, lifting her chin from her hands.

Al shifted on the bed, looking back to the jersey spread across his legs. "Perhaps. There was certainly something important about her."

The three of them sat in silence for a moment. Just an hour ago, Nolie had been in her bedroom, reading and thinking that the next day, she might go check out that ruined castle on the hill.

Now she was standing in Bel's bedroom with a boy from 1918 who was telling them that they had to light a magic lighthouse to keep fog from eating the village.

Before she could ask Albert any more questions, though, there was another knock at the door.

"Nolie?" Bel's mum called. "I'll drive you back now."

Sighing, Nolie thrust her hands in her hair. "Okay," she called out. "We're coming."

Then she turned to Bel and Al. "So for now, Albert can go back to the caves. Tomorrow, we'll see if we can sneak him somewhere less damp and deadly, and also free of girls."

"And then what?" Bel whispered, her hazel eyes wide.

Nolie stood up. "And then we'll figure out what to do next."

From "The Sad Tale of Cait McInnish,"
Chapter 13,
Legends of the North

AND SO ON ONE BRIGHT, COLD DAY, CAIT WAS TAKEN to the water's edge and put into a rowboat. The wind had teeth that bit through the simple shift she wore, the water so cold it seemed to burn when it touched her bare feet.

The laird's men were in another boat, tied to hers with a rope, and they rowed her out into the gray water while her stomach churned like the waves. They were just off the small rocky outcrop where, years before, men from her village had built a lighthouse, when the laird's men untied the rope from her boat and rowed away again.

Her own small boat creaked and Cait shivered, smelling salt and sea and stone. Overhead, the light in the lighthouse flickered, and she stared at that bit of flame. Her father had helped build the lighthouse, had been the first to light the beacon. This is what Cait's family had done for the village, and the village had still left her to drown or starve or go mad with thirst all the same.

Cait did not believe in magic, but there must have been some magic in her veins. Or if there was not, perhaps her heart was so broken that something dark was able to slither through the cracks.

She stared at that flame until her eyes burned, until her hands, still tied behind her back, began to tingle.

And the flame went out.

CHAPTER 15

"I FEEL LIKE THE HAT MIGHT BE A BIT MUCH."

Bel frowned as she said it, studying Al from the other side of the tearoom table. He'd stayed at the caves last night, and they'd met him on the beach earlier, bringing him into the village for lunch. Before he'd left the night before, Bel had managed to sneak a few things from her kitchen, but some apples, string cheese, and a few granola bars weren't a real meal.

They were planning on moving him into the Institute's attic later today, and as such, Nolie had thought he'd needed a better disguise than Simon's old clothes. Hence the baseball cap she'd found for him somewhere in the Institute, which would've been fine had it not had a plush Loch Ness monster attached to it. Nessie's head stuck out over the bill of the cap while her tail poked out in the back, making it look like Al had a sea serpent swimming through his head.

Nolie looked over at him as she used the side of her fork to cut a hunk out of her piece of chocolate cake. "What? No, it makes him look like a *tourist*, Bel. He's blending in."

Al scowled slightly, casting his eyes upward even though he couldn't actually see the bright green head with its googly eyes. "I don't know what a tourist is, but they must be mad silly things to wear caps such as these."

They'd decided to have lunch at the tearoom today since, as Nolie pointed out, that's where all the tourists went, so it would help with Al's "hidden in plain sight" thing. It wasn't a bad idea—the place was pretty full of unfamiliar people, all with cameras or backpacks—but Bel was beginning to think Nolie had suggested it mostly for the cake.

Al seemed pleased with the food, too, tucking into a bowl of carrot soup and an egg-and-cress sandwich. It was gray today, with the smell of rain in the air, and Bel wrapped her fingers around a Styrofoam cup of tea. She'd made one for Al and Nolie, too. Al's was plain because that's what he liked, but she'd put loads of milk and sugar in hers and Nolie's. Breathing in the sweet steam from her cup now, she rested her heels on the rung of her chair.

Leslie's family ran the tearoom, so Bel hadn't ventured

in ever since their . . . whatever it was that'd happened. Strange how with Al and Nolie at her table, it hadn't given her pause to come in today, though.

Of course, that might have been because she had more pressing things on her mind than why Leslie Douglas didn't like her anymore.

"Was this a tearoom when you were alive?" Nolie asked Al, and he paused in demolishing his own slice of cake to glance around.

"No, it was a shop."

He seemed more interested in eating his cake than giving them further details, but Bel still said, "My family owns a shop. We'll take—"

She stopped, her face feeling warm. She'd been about to promise to take him by the shop after lunch, but how could she? His face was on the back wall, and, Nessie hat or no, Bel felt fairly certain her mum would think he looked familiar. Also, she wasn't sure she wanted to explain the memorial to Al.

Nolie looked over at her, eyebrows raised, but Bel just shook her head and took another sip of tea.

The three of them sat there in silence for a bit, and Bel was beginning to think Al would just eat all the cake in the tearoom in silence when he suddenly said, "The fog took the shop."

Bel sat her cup down with a thump, sloshing some tea over the side. "What?"

He kept shoveling in cake, the Nessie head bobbing. "When it started coming closer. Got all the way up to here, and the shop vanished." Then he raised his head and looked around. "Pretty sure it didn't come back once I'd lit the light. This place doesn't look the same." He wrinkled his brow, dark eyes searching the walls.

Like Gifts from the End of the World, the Foghorn Tearoom had been designed mostly to appeal to visitors, so there were green-and-blue plaid curtains in the windows, photographs of the Boundary on the walls, a few posters of other pretty spots in Scotland. Even the placemats were plaid, and bagpipe music drifted from little speakers in the corner.

Back when Bel and Leslie were friends, it had been one of Bel's favorite places to come, and not just because Leslie's mum's chocolate cake was so good. It always smelled nice, the earthy scent of tea in the air, the sweet smell of baking drifting out of the kitchen. Especially on a cold gray day like today when the sea just beyond the window looked like stone, and drops of mist seemed to hover in the air.

Nolie had finished her cake, and was looking out toward the sea now. "The fog came in this far?" she asked. "All the way up here?"

They could just barely see the Boundary from here, and it was almost impossible to believe that it had once slid this far inland.

It *was* impossible. It had to be. Fog could move, of course it could, but it didn't *take* things.

Bel said that now, and both Nolie and Al looked at her.

"You really want to start calling things 'impossible' when you're having lunch with a dead kid?" Nolie asked, and for once, Al didn't argue with her.

Sighing, Bel sat forward, her nails digging little crescent moons into her cup. "There could be some . . . I don't know, scientific properties in the fog, preserving him. *That* I can believe. But the fog coming in closer, and taking *buildings*? Then going back because someone lit a magical lighthouse light?" She shook her head. "Wouldn't we know? Wouldn't there be stories?"

"They were probably sad. And ashamed," Al said quietly. He was stirring a spoon in his soup, looking out the window. "The year I left, Journey's End sent six people into the fog, and they never came back."

If it meant saving the village, would people send someone out into the fog now? Bel chewed her bottom lip, thinking about it. She wanted to say that no, of course they wouldn't, but then she thought of Jaime with his bright eyes and quick smile.

He'd go, she realized. In a heartbeat.

The door opened, and with it a gust of cool, damp air, and then Leslie was standing there, the hood of her slicker pulled up over her brown hair, and as always, Cara and Alice right behind.

When Leslie's eyes met Bel's, Bel wished she could suddenly become invisible. It was one thing to see Leslie out and about, but here, in her family's own tearoom, there wasn't anywhere to hide, or any way to avoid her, really.

Al and Nolie had clearly picked up on the tension, Nolie looking over at the three girls, and Al lifting his shoulders a little, like if he could just make his neck low enough, no one would notice his hat.

But Leslie had noticed, all right, and she and the other two girls came over to the table, the soles of their trainers squeaking on the hardwood floor. "Hiya, Bel," Leslie said, and Bel gave her a weak smile.

"Hiya."

"Haven't seen you much this summer," Leslie continued, and Bel fought the urge to snap, "More like haven't *spoken* to me much," and instead just gave a little shrug.

"Busy at the shop."

She wished Leslie would just go away now, and she could feel Nolie's eyes on her, asking a million questions.

But then Alice stepped forward. She was taller than Leslie, with the same dark, straight hair, although her eyes were blue, not brown like Leslie's. They were also kind of mean as she glanced down beside Nolie's plate and saw her book.

"*Monsters of the Minch*," she read out loud, and behind her, Cara gave a muffled giggle.

Leslie just shifted her weight from one foot to the other.

Alice looked over at Al then, and his hat. "Aaaaand a Nessie cap," she drawled. "The two of you planning to go hunting for fairies after your tea?"

Bel's face was burning now, and there were two spots of red high on Al's cheekbones.

Nolie turned her face up to Alice and smiled. "Why? *Are* there fairies around here?"

Alice scowled, then flicked her gaze over at Bel. "I thought you weren't supposed to make friends with tourists," she said, her voice almost sneering. "Isn't that what you told Leslie?"

Bel's eyes flew to Leslie, and she watched her former friend squirm slightly, not meeting Bel's gaze. Was that it, then? Sure, when Leslie had first started hanging out around Alice, Bel had mentioned her mum's advice, about how people not from Journey's End never stayed long, but she'd only said it because she didn't want Leslie to get her feelings hurt.

And yeah, maybe she'd been a *bit* jealous, but she hadn't meant that Leslie *couldn't* be friends with Alice.

But none of that seemed to matter now, because it was clear Alice had already made up her mind about Bel.

"Anyway," Alice said, backing away from the table. "Have fun monster hunting or whatever. Come on, I'm not hungry after all."

The three girls drifted back toward the door, Leslie shooting Bel one last, unreadable look before they were gone.

Al, Bel, and Nolie sat in silence.

"They seem fun," Nolie said at last. "And by fun, I mean 'the worst.'"

"Leslie wasn't all that bad," Bel muttered, looking into her tea. It had gone cold now, the sugar at the bottom a kind of brownish sludge, and she frowned at her cup before standing up to toss it in the bin.

"We need to get Al into the Institute attic while your dad's still in Wythe," she told Nolie. "Then I have to get back to the shop."

Nolie and Al were both still watching her, but neither of them argued as they cleaned up the table, then set off into the misty afternoon.

Bel and Nolie both had rain jackets, but Al just hunched his shoulders against the drizzle, eyes narrowing a bit.

"At least this beastie should be happy in weather like this," he said, flicking Nessie's head with his finger, and Bel glanced around. The city center was nearly deserted, and there were a ton of cheap plastic (and plaid) ponchos at the shop. "Go stand under that awning," she told Nolie and Al, pointing to the covering above the tiny Journey's End museum.

They did as she'd asked, and Bel quickly jogged across the street to Gifts from the End of the World, digging her key out of her pocket.

But as she glanced up, something taped to the window on the door caught her eye. It was a plain white sheet of paper, which she snatched down and unfolded.

It was a note, and it was only a few lines, scrawled in a scratchy handwriting that made Bel think of spiderwebs.

If you want answers, I have them. Meet me at the manor house. Sunset.

And under that was a name.

M. McLeod.

M.

Maggie.

CHAPTER 16

"SCOTLAND IS INVOLVING A LOT LESS PLAID THAN I thought," Nolie said as she stood by the ice cream truck with Albert, waiting for him to make his choice. The fact that there were over a dozen different kinds of ice cream was blowing his mind a little bit, and Nolie didn't want to rush him.

"And no one has offered me haggis," she went on. "Which I guess is a good thing."

"Haggis is lovely," Albert replied, and then finally said to the ice cream man, "One vanilla cone, please."

He carefully handed over the money Bel had given him, and Nolie smiled at the look of wonder on his face as he took a bite of the soft-serve cone.

They were meant to meet Maggie at sunset, but in Scotland in the summer, that was a lot later than Nolie had reckoned. She'd been surprised when Bel had said they'd meet on the path to Maggie's at a little after nine, but getting out had been easier than she'd hoped—her dad was pretty focused on Institute Stuff right now—and there were actually a few kids her age milling around the village. Heck, even the ice cream truck stayed open late.

Once Albert had his cone, they made their way up the hill that led away from Journey's End, off toward the gentle green slopes overlooking the ocean. "This is brilliant, this is!" Albert enthused, waving his ice cream cone at Nolie. "And right off a lorry! Frozen and everything."

"Yeah, the twenty-first century is super rad," Nolie muttered, her eyes off to the side, looking at that tall cliff. At the thick bank of fog hanging over the steel-gray water.

"Super rad," Albert repeated slowly, and Nolie smiled. His accent, like Bel's, did all sorts of funny things to words. The S twisted behind his teeth, the R rolled like a wave on the shore.

The wind had ruffled his hair, and in his Midlothian Hearts jersey and sweatpants, he should have looked like any regular boy. But even in sneakers, there was something different about Albert. Nolie wondered if she was the only one who could feel it.

"Is it easier today?" she asked, turning up the collar of her jacket as the wind blew harder. "The whole 'being in the future now' thing?"

Albert crunched into his cone, mulling that over. "A

bit," he finally said, swallowing. "The village seems the same in a lot of ways. There are still shops and places to get tea. Although I haven't seen anyone walking a cow down the high street yet," he added, and Nolie laughed.

"I'll see if I can't make that happen at some point," she told him, turning to walk backward. "Make you feel at home."

Al smiled back. "It is loud, though. In the village. Mostly the automobiles." Shaking his head, he ate the last bit of cone before saying, "I dinna know how you all stand it, that constant clatter. But you two were right—I do like the clothes."

Grinning, he looked down at himself, tugging his jersey out a bit so that he could read the front of it. "Much more comfortable. And the shoes are—what's that word?"

"Ace," Nolie supplied, and Albert nodded, lifting one foot and admiring his sneakers. She had no idea where Bel had unearthed them, and they did look a little big, but they were better than nothing.

"Ace," Al echoed. "Super rad. Super ace rad."

Nolie laughed and shook her head. "Super ace rad," she repeated, and Al turned his smile on her.

"And you too are Super Ace Rad, Nolie Stanhope."

Nolie wasn't sure why, but that made her face suddenly feel hot in spite of the wind. Now that Albert was dressed like a regular boy, she couldn't help noticing that he was . . . well, he was cute. He had nice dark eyes, and all that thick black hair, and when he smiled, his nose kind of crinkled at the bridge in a way she liked.

She turned her head, pretending to look at something off in the distance, and hoped Al wouldn't notice her blush.

Maybe Al felt weird, too, because he cleared his throat and fidgeted with the sleeves of his jersey.

"What would you have said instead of 'ace' or 'rad' back in your time?" she asked, tugging at the hem of her jacket.

Albert ruffled his hair, thinking. "S'pose it's the same as top-hole?" he said. "That's what I would've called that ice cream or those shoes. Top-hole."

Nolie giggled, shaking her head. "That's *awful*," she said, and Albert gave an easy shrug.

"I'd agree 'ace' is better," he said. "Or sometimes, if something was really grand, we'd call it 'wizard.'"

"Okay, that I like," Nolie said with a decisive nod. "Wizard. That's good. Very Harry Potter."

"Who's he?" Albert asked, his face scrunched up, and Nolie just laughed.

"What do you think she wants with us?" Nolie asked, changing the subject. "Maggie."

"Dunno," he said, shoving his hands into his pockets, "Hoping it's some kind of answer about why I'm here instead of home, and why that light is so ruddy important."

"I'd guess because it keeps man-eating fog away?" Nolie suggested. "That sounds 'ruddy important' to me."

Albert threw her a smile over his shoulder. "You and Bel are very different, you know that?"

Nolie rolled her eyes, tugging her jacket tighter around her. The wind up here seemed to find ways of slithering in despite her jeans and long-sleeved shirt. "Well, yeah," she said. "We're different people. Were all girls the same when you were ... here?"

Now Albert blushed a little, or maybe that was just the wind. "Didna really talk to girls," he said, his shoulders creeping up near his ears. "It wasn't the done thing, talking with a girl once you were older than ten or so."

Nolie stopped in her tracks, staring at Albert. "What, so you couldn't be friends with a girl without your families wanting you to marry them? Even when you were just twelve?"

Albert stopped, too, turning around to scowl at her. "No, that isna what I meant. It's just that girls do other things. They were learning to keep a house, while we were leaning to fish or farm. We wouldna had anything to talk about had we been friends."

Folding her arms, Nolie stared him down. "So girls were boring?"

The tips of Albert's ears were bright pink now. "I didna say that!" he insisted, and luckily, at that moment, Bel

157

came jogging up the hill, her sandy hair bright against the gray sky, still waving a green scarf over her head, like they wouldn't know it was her without it or something.

It made Nolie laugh, and for the moment, she decided to let Albert slide on his whole "didn't hang out with girls" thing. Seriously, had boys always been like this? Just last year, one of her friends from school, Ethan, had decided they had to stop playing video games online together because "it looks weird." And since Ethan had cut his own bangs back in second grade, Nolie wasn't so sure he was one to talk about what looked weird.

"There you are!" she said to Bel now.

"Sorry!" Bel called, a little breathless as she joined them on the path. "For once, Jaime and Jack were both behaving themselves, so Mum wanted to hang out with me for a bit. Took me ages to get away."

Nolie waved, then turned to the manor house, which was standing on a slight rise. It couldn't have looked more like a place where people got horribly murdered—maybe because people *had* been horribly murdered there. Weren't people always fighting over big houses? It seemed likely that at least *once*, someone here must have taken an arrow to the eyeball or something.

"So . . . we're doing this?" she asked Bel and Albert. "Just knocking on the door and being like, 'Hi, we got your note, here we are'?"

Albert had his hands in his pockets and was already walking up to the house.

"Seems the only way," he said, and Bel followed. Nolie looked up at the ruined castle, its jagged stones tearing up toward the cloudy sky.

"Super ace rad," she muttered as she started walking, and Bel looked back at her, eyebrows raised.

"What did you just say?"

Shaking her head, Nolie thrust her hands into the pockets of her jacket, mimicking Al's pose. "Nothing," she said, and then she nearly tripped over a loose stone.

When she'd first seen the house through the telescope at the Institute, it had looked spooky, definitely. Bel's story about the old castle being struck by lightning had been even spookier, and Nolie fought the urge to grin as they made their way past the rubble. There were still a few piles of stones that gave the suggestion of towers, but for the most part, it was all a ruin, and Nolie reached for her notebook. She knew Bel and Albert were taking this pretty seriously, which meant that now probably wasn't the time for her to give in to ghosty nerdery, so she tried to make her face look as expressionless as possible.

There was definitely a weird feeling in the air, and she wrote that down, along with the fact that all the hairs on her arms were standing up. That might just have been due to the wind and the setting sun, but still, couldn't be *sure* it wasn't proof of an electromagnetic field.

Writing down a quick description of the castle helped, too, since it meant Nolie was focused on that, and not on how much closer the house was getting.

It was just a plain stone building, some moss growing in the cracks between the stones, but the rows of windows were all dark, like sightless eyes.

Next to her, Bel was pulling out the note, and Nolie wondered if she meant to hold it up to Maggie as proof of why they were here. Although, looking at that dark house, Nolie wasn't sure Maggie was even home, and a little part of her hoped she wasn't. It would be nice to go back to civilization, maybe go back to Bel's warm, chaotic house and have a cup of tea.

But no. That's not what Gary and Bess from *Spirit Chasers* would do.

That in mind, Nolie pushed her shoulders back and walked up the shallow stone steps to the house. It seemed to loom over her, and everything was in soft purple shadows now. The wind whipped through her hair, and she tucked it back behind her ears with one hand while, with the other, she lifted the massive iron ring on the door and knocked.

CHAPTER 17

BEL STOOD AT THE BASE OF THE STEPS, STARING UP AT Maggie McLeod's house. She'd never been all that spooked by scary houses before—you couldn't throw a rock in the Highlands without hitting a ruined castle, it seemed—but there was something about this house up close that gave her a case of the shivers.

Maybe it was all those windows reflecting the setting sun, or how lonely the house seemed, perched on top of its hill. Maybe it was the way the wind sounded blowing through the leaves of the one stubby tree off to just one side.

Or maybe it was knowing that if Mum found out she'd gone banging on Mrs. McLeod's door at ten o'clock at night, Bel would be in the worst trouble of her life.

There were no sounds coming from inside the house; all she could hear was the hollow sound of the wind blowing. And then Bel thought she heard something like a laugh. A giggle, really, from somewhere behind them.

She turned, looking over her shoulder, but there was nothing there except for the piles of stone from the old castle, now just black lumps in the gloom.

Nolie knocked again, and the sound seemed to echo around them. Next to Bel, Al was standing straight, looking more like the boy in his photograph than he had earlier.

Probably because he'd ditched the Loch Ness monster cap.

"It seems like she isn't home?" he suggested to Nolie now, but Nolie just screwed up her face, still holding the note Bel had found.

"She's really old," she told Al. "It probably takes her a while to get to the door."

And just as she'd finished saying that, the door creaked open, Maggie McLeod standing there in her jeans and a bright blue jumper. "Not so old that my hearing has gone, lassie," she said to Nolie, who flushed as red as her hair.

This close, Maggie did look old. *Really* old. Her skin was papery thin and her white hair bright in the light of a lamp behind her.

"Now what are you doing on my doorstep at this hour, Bel McKissick?"

Bel was so surprised that Maggie knew her name that for a moment, she didn't say anything.

Luckily, Nolie was there to take the lead. Snatching the

note from Bel, she thrust it at Maggie, her hand wavering just a little bit.

"We're here because of this," she said, and Maggie took the paper with thin fingers, holding it up close to her face to read the writing.

"What on earth," she said softly, then lowered the note with a snap. "I didn't write this."

Her pale blue eyes narrowed. "What are you on about, girls?" she asked, her lips pursing slightly. "Think it's funny to play jokes on old ladies?"

"We weren't," Bel said, stepping back a bit. The night was getting darker, and she suddenly wished they'd never come up here. If Mrs. McLeod knew who she was, she might tell her mum. "We just found the note, and we—we had some questions, so we thought you might know something."

"About what?" Maggie asked, still glaring at them, and Bel was about to spill the whole story of the fog and the lighthouse, and maybe even Al himself, crazy as it would sound, when suddenly, Mrs. McLeod leaned forward a little. "Who are *you?*" she demanded.

Bel looked around. She hadn't realized that Al had backed up into the shadows a little, but now he moved forward, his shoulders straight.

Maggie was staring at him, one hand clutching the doorframe. "I know you," she said slowly. "I'm sure of it. I—"

Then there was a burst of giggles from behind them, followed by a bunch of frantic shushing, and Maggie drew back, her lips clamping shut again.

"Play your pranks on other people, all of you," she said, and with that, the door slammed shut in their faces.

Bel could only stand there for a moment, frozen, but Nolie had no such problems, apparently. She stomped down the front steps and close to the nearest ruined tower, where the giggles had come from.

"Seriously?" she said, and a large shadow rose up from behind the pile of rocks. Then the shadow split into three parts—Alice, Cara, and Leslie.

Bel wasn't sure whether the heat in her face came from anger or embarrassment. Might have been a little bit of both.

"So you're too good for people who aren't from Journey's End, but you'll take a couple of tourists witch hunting," Alice said, her face smug in the dim light. "Classic."

Then she looked over at Leslie. "I told you she was weird about us being friends."

Leslie was fidgeting, pulling at the ends of her hair, and like always, she wouldn't look at Bel. It made Bel wonder if she did that so she could pretend none of this was happening, that she wasn't just standing there while Alice was being a jerk.

"I wasn't," Bel said. "I just didn't want her to get her feelings hurt, and—"

"*And*," Nolie broke in, "we were doing something *important*. We're trying to keep your stupid village from being eaten, and you are *wasting our time*."

Alice stared at Nolie for a second, blinking, and then she laughed. A big laugh, loud and mean.

"Being eaten? By what, another monster?" Alice looked around, her brown hair swinging over her shoulders. "Where's your friend with his hat? Shouldn't he be the one warning us about monsters?"

Bel realized that Al was nowhere around, and while that was not great, for now, she just wanted to get Nolie away from Alice.

"If this place *does* get eaten by killer fog, I hope it gets you first," Nolie said, and Alice rolled her eyes.

"Okay, sure, killer fog. Got it. Did you read that in one of your books?"

"I read it in your face," Nolie muttered back, and while that was maybe the worst comeback in the history of ever, Bel still appreciated the attempt.

"Come on," she said, taking Nolie's arm and steering her back the way they'd come. "Let's go home."

They walked away in the darkness, and Bel was glad for the moonlight that kept them from tripping over rocks.

"We would've gotten *something* from her," Nolie said as they carefully made their way down the hill. There was a dark shape moving in front of them that Bel was pretty sure was Al, so they hurried to catch up.

"She recognized Albert," Nolie went on. "Or seemed to. But now she thinks we're jerk kids who are mean to old ladies, so we'll never get to talk to her. Ugh."

Ugh was right.

By the time they caught up with Al, Bel's teeth were chattering a little. The wind coming off the ocean was colder than usual for June, it seemed like, and Al had his hands shoved in his pockets, his shoulders up to his ears.

"Hey!" Nolie called as they caught up. "Why did you hurry off?"

He shrugged, uncomfortable. "Didn't expect her to recognize me," he said. "It felt funny."

Bel nearly tripped over a loose stone, and Nolie caught her shoulder, keeping her from face planting.

"Did you recognize *her*?" she asked Al, and he shook his head.

"No," he said, and then walked on.

The girls watched him go, and then, after a moment, Nolie said, "I think he's lying."

Bel sighed. "Me too."

CHAPTER 18

"DOES THIS MAKE MY HEAD LOOK BIG?" NOLIE ASKED THE next day, plopping a plastic Viking helmet on her head.

Bel had been sitting at the counter, staring out the window, but now she glanced over and laughed, just like Nolie had been hoping she would.

"Aye, a wee bit," she said, but then her smile faded and she went back to staring.

Sighing, Nolie took off the helmet and put it back on the display. It was quiet in the shop now, but they were waiting for the boat to come back. Just fifteen minutes ago, the shop had been so crowded, Nolie had finally decided to hide in the storage space behind the restrooms. She'd gotten spoiled, having the shop and Bel to herself so often, but this had been a busy week in Journey's End. News of the fog inching closer had gotten out, and either people wanted to see it before the Institute shut down tourism, or they had some kind of morbid desire to get close to something dangerous. "Maybe a hairy coo hat would be better?" she mused, picking up the hat in question. It was made to look like the big, woolly cattle people raised up in this part of Scotland, complete with shaggy orange fur and long horns. Nolie put it on and it slipped down, blocking her vision.

When she pushed it back up, Bel wasn't even looking at her, and Nolie bit back another sigh.

"So . . . I can keep trying on silly hats, or you can just tell me what you're thinking," she said, and Bel gave a sigh of her own, tucking her hair behind her ears.

"Yesterday," she said, letting that word be the only explanation, and Nolie suddenly understood, nodding.

"Right. When your friends were jerks."

"They're not my friends," Bel said quickly, and then propped her elbows on the glass counter, her chin in her hands. "Well, not all of 'em. Leslie was, though. We were best friends, really, proper mates."

Nolie managed to keep her face serious, which was pretty impressive seeing as how "mates" sounded funny to her. "So that Alice girl moved here, and that's when everything went wrong?"

Glumly, Bel nodded. "Aye. Her dad moved from Wythe to open an arcade here, and maybe Leslie thinks hanging out with someone whose family owns a place like *that* is cooler than hanging out with a girl whose family owns a shop."

She sounded so sad that Nolie suddenly really wanted to kick Alice. Even yesterday's prank hadn't bothered her so much. It had been a jerk move and everything, but hey, creeping around the manor house at sunset had been fun, and nothing bad had happened. Besides, people couldn't laugh at you if you were laughing first.

"Well, I don't know what kind of arcade Alice's family runs," Nolie said, taking a few of the stuffed sheep from their display and lining them up on the counter. "But it could never be as cool as a place that sells *these* bad boys. So Alice and her video games are *bums*. And I mean that in the butt sense."

Bel let out a spluttering laugh, covering her mouth with one hand. But then she lowered it and grinned at Nolie. "*Such* bums." But after a moment, her smile faded. "It wasn't just them, though. The bums." She made a frustrated sound and once again propped her chin in her hand. "I thought Maggie might have actually told us something. All of this seems so mad, and there's Al and the Boundary, and all of it, and it just seemed like someone was finally handing us an important piece of the puzzle, you know?"

Nolie was still wearing the cow hat, and she fiddled with the horns as she thought that over. For her, this whole thing had just been fun. Scary at times, sure, and there was no doubt that Albert was the weirdest thing to ever happen in her life, but nothing about it made her *sad*. It almost felt like being in a story, like something that was happening to other people.

But this was Bel's town, where she lived and her family worked, and maybe the idea of the fog creeping up was freaking her out a lot more than she'd let on. And honestly, maybe it would be Nolie's town, too? Not all the time, of course—she'd still be heading back to Georgia in August. But it definitely seemed like her dad had plans to put down roots here, and that would make this an important place to Nolie, too.

Tugging the hat off, Nolie said, "So the Maggie thing went bust. Maybe someone else knows what's going on. Or maybe Albert's wrong, and the fog isn't going to do that whole 'town-eating' thing. It's moving closer, but not by, like, a lot? Maybe what's happening this time is different."

Bel nodded, but Nolie didn't think she really believed her.

"And my mum caught me coming back in," Bel added on a sigh. "So she was mad at me. Or disappointed, I guess, which is worse."

Now *that* was something Nolie understood perfectly. "You could tell her it was my fault," she suggested. "Blame it on my terrible American influence."

Bel snorted, twirling a strand of hair around her finger. "I think she would've called your dad, but with everything that happened at the Institute, it would probably be too awkward."

Putting the hat back on its rack, Nolie pulled out her phone, checking the time.

"Albert was supposed to meet us here at noon," she said. "And it's almost twelve twenty."

"Does he even have a watch?" Bel asked, sitting up on the stool behind the counter. It was sunny for once, and a shaft of sunlight fell across the glass display of spoons, flashing in Nolie's eyes.

"Yeah, I gave him mine since I could use my phone. It's bright purple plastic, but he didn't seem to mind."

"Maybe he's just running late?" Bel asked, but Nolie chewed her lower lip, looking out the window and hoping to see Albert jogging up the street.

There were plenty of people out and about today, but none of them were a slender dark-haired boy in ill-fitting clothes.

"You don't think . . ." Nolie started, but she didn't want to finish the sentence. Didn't want to think it, even. Albert had been really quiet on their walk back from Maggie's the night before, clearly thinking something over. What if he had decided to take matters into his own hands, to row the *Selkie* back out to the Boundary himself to light the light?

When she looked over at Bel, she could tell her friend

was thinking the same thing, and without saying a word, Bel hopped off the stool, opened the door to the shop, and turned the sign to CLOSED.

Nolie followed behind her, realizing that Bel was heading toward the beach.

Dang it, Albert, Nolie thought, stuffing her hands in her pockets. *Please don't be as stupid as I think you might have been.*

They were both almost running now, passing the truck that sold fish and chips, the little bookshop, the weird candle place that always smelled like smoke. Just off to the right, there was the arcade Bel had mentioned, and Nolie glanced at it, noticing Beattie's Game Stop written on a sign in big green letters. There was a giant window at the front of the arcade, and Nolie could see all the lights from the games inside.

And then she saw something else.

Stopping in her tracks, she grabbed Bel's jacket, pulling the other girl up short.

"Holy. Hairy. Coo."

CHAPTER 19

BEL HAD ACCEPTED THAT LIFE IN JOURNEY'S END WAS getting weirder by the second, but that still hadn't prepared her for the sight of Albert MacLeish—Al, the dark-eyed dead boy at the back of her family's shop—jumping around on a brightly lit machine called *Dance Your Pants Off USA.*

And yet when she walked into the arcade, Nolie just behind her, there he was, in her brother Simon's sweatpants and Midlothian Hearts jersey, following the movements on the screen, his feet landing on circles of colored lights.

Beside her, Nolie burst into giggles, covering the lower half of her face with her hands. "Oh, this is *excellent*," she all but squealed. "Look at him!"

Bel couldn't really *not* look at him. Everyone in the arcade was, because Al was—to use a Nolie-ism—"killing it." His hair was slicked back with sweat, the jersey sticking to his back, but he was grinning, and when Bel looked over to the side of the machine, she saw Leslie and Alice watching him and smiling, too.

All right, bad enough that Al had apparently forgotten all about lying low, but the way Alice and Leslie were looking at him?

That was *beyond* not okay. They were the ones who found Al, after all, not Alice and Leslie.

"We have to stop him," she hissed to Nolie, who, still beaming with delight, didn't take her eyes off Al.

"No way," Nolie said. "I'm imprinting this on my brain forever. Our very own 1918 boy, showing us how it's done. Besides, we can't stop him now. He's about to beat the high score!"

Sure enough, the lighted numbers on the display were showing that Al was close to scoring 30,000 points, the highest being 33,000.

"The machine came with that score," Bel told her, tugging Nolie forward. "No one here ever uses it, because it's so embarrassing."

"Those dance machines are kind of old news," Nolie agreed, but Bel shook her head.

"No, it's not that, it's . . . it's the *name*."

"*Dance Your Pants Off USA?*" Nolie asked, raising her eyebrows. In the weird lighting of the arcade, her hair looked purple, and her freckles stood out even more.

"Exactly," Bel said, and Nolie laughed, but let herself

be pulled toward the group of kids—both local and tourists—who were now watching Al thrust his arms out to the side before taking a few quicks steps back, then forward.

"I don't think anyone is going to actually dance their pants off, Bel," Nolie said. "So the people of Journey's End shouldn't be that scandalized by it."

Bel realized what the problem was.

"No, over here, pants doesn't mean those," she said, nodding at Nolie's jeans. "*Those* are trousers. Here, pants mean—"

Dropping her voice, she leaned closer and said, "It means *underwear*."

When the machine had first gone up in the arcade, there had been about a million jokes about it in school, and no one would dare to dance on it for fear of a million *more* jokes being made.

But Nolie just threw her head back and laughed again, a big laugh this time. "Okay, okay," she said when she could finally catch her breath. "As soon as Albert gets off that thing, we have *got* to tell him. He'll *die*. I mean. Again, I guess."

Rolling her eyes, Bel moved closer to the machine and Al. There were about a dozen kids around him, most of whom she recognized from school. When she accidentally nudged Brian Fitzroy, he glanced over at her.

"This lad is *brilliant*," he enthused, and Bel nodded weakly. Brian's family owned the chippie truck that was usually parked just outside Gifts from the End of the World. Like Bel, Brian helped his family out from time to time, and he'd been in Bel's shop loads of times. What if he'd looked closely at the pictures? What if any second now, he recognized this "brilliant lad"?

But Nolie was right. Believing such a thing seemed so weird that even if someone *had* noticed the resemblance, they probably wouldn't piece it together.

The bright red numbers ticked past 33,000, and the little crowd around Al cheered. Finally, the song came to an end, and he stopped, resting his hands on the bars on either side of the platform, hanging his head down and taking deep breaths.

Bel was suddenly afraid he'd overdone it. He might *look* like a regular thirteen-year-old kid, but he was actually a hundred and eleven years old.

What if his heart was bad or something? Or he had arthritis?

But when Al lifted his head again, he was still smiling, and it was such a good smile that Bel felt herself grinning back.

There was a piercing whistle just behind her, and she turned to see Nolie with her index fingers stuck in her mouth. Al smiled even broader at that, and as he hopped down, he saw Bel.

"Yer not mad, are ye?" he asked, out of breath, and Bel glanced around at the kids near them. They were already moving on to other things now that the show was over, but Alice and Leslie were still watching pretty closely, Alice propping her hands on her hips.

"Kind of?" she told him. "Mostly because we told you not to draw attention to yourself, and then you *danced for a crowd of people.*"

Al rolled his shoulders. "I felt cooped up in the attic," he told her. "And I had a bit of extra time before I needed to meet you and Nolie, so I thought I'd have a wander, and then I saw this place."

He looked around with wide eyes, his hands open at his sides, like he could hardly take in the glory that was Beattie's Game Spot. "How d'ye keep from spending every moment of yer day in here?"

Bel's eyes fell on the grimy old video game machines, the basketball hoop with part of its net hanging off, the grubby carpet underneath her feet.

But then she tried to see it from Al's point of view. "What did you even do for fun back in your time?"

"Chase sheep?" Nolie guessed, and Al shot her a look before glancing down at the carpet, shrugging.

"Possible we did that a time or two," he confessed. "But if you could catch one, then Frances May would—" He stopped there, his face going red, and Nolie widened her eyes.

"Wait, would some girl kiss you for catching sheep?"

"Don't want to talk about it," Al mumbled, and Bel shook her head, needing to get this conversation back on track.

"Where did you even get money for this place?" she asked Al now.

"Oh," Nolie said, edging forward. "Um. That might be my bad? But my dad gives me way too much 'daily spending money,' and I thought Albert might not want to have to depend on us every time he wants to get ice cream from the truck."

"Which is all the time," Al added with a nod. "That ice cream is super ace rad."

Despite herself, Bel laughed. "Okay, for the last time, that is *not* something people say. Now let's get you out of here before someone recognizes—"

"Bel?"

Bel turned to see Leslie standing there, fiddling with the end of her long, dark braid. "Hi," was all she said, and Bel felt that squirmy feeling start up in her stomach again.

"Hi."

The lighting that had made Nolie look extra freckled

made Leslie look really pale, and Bel almost felt sorry for her. She seemed so uncomfortable standing there without Alice or Cara behind her, facing Nolie and Al.

"I'm sorry," she blurted out suddenly, and Bel was so surprised that all she could say was, "Oh."

"About yesterday," Leslie went on. She was shifting her weight, her fingers playing along the edges of her sleeves. "It was mean, and stupid, and I don't know why we did it."

"To be mean and stupid?" Nolie offered, and Leslie gave her a stricken look.

Waving Nolie off, Bel said, "Aye, it was. But it's over now, and we're none the worse for it, so . . ."

In the silence that followed, Leslie continued to fidget with her braid while Nolie stood with her arms crossed next to Bel.

As for Bel? She didn't know *what* to think.

Apparently awkward silence was too much for Al, because he cleared his throat, and Leslie's eyes lifted to his face. She tilted her head to one side.

"I know you, right? It's been bothering me since we saw you at the tearoom."

Of course Al would look familiar to Leslie. She'd spent a lot of time at the shop before everything had gone pear-shaped over the spring. She might have even helped dust his picture a time or two.

But before Leslie could look any closer, Nolie grabbed

Al's arm and started tugging him toward the door. "He's my cousin," she said. "And, um, he has a YouTube channel. You've probably seen him there. Okay, bye!"

"What's YouTube?" Bel heard Al ask Nolie as she dragged him away, and Leslie blinked.

"I should go," Bel said, jerking her thumb after Al and Nolie. "Get back to the shop. My mum wasn't happy about me being gone the other night."

It probably wasn't very nice, but Bel still liked the flicker of guilt that crossed Leslie's face. Served her right, playing a prank like that.

But then Bel remembered that Leslie didn't know about the fog or what Al claimed was coming, so she couldn't have understood just how disappointed Bel felt when she realized there wasn't any help coming from Maggie.

Still, she just gave Leslie one last look, unsure of what else to say before jogging after Al and Nolie.

They were both outside the arcade, and Al had somehow already gotten another ice cream cone. When Bel looked at Nolie, Nolie nodded across the way to where the ice lolly lorry was parked.

"I think it's following him," she said. "Knows he's an easy sale."

Al was still sweaty—Bel hoped there was a shower he could sneak into at the Institute—but he seemed happier than Bel had seen him since they'd met, leaning against the side of the arcade, eating his ice cream. She remembered the panic she'd felt realizing they couldn't find him, afraid he'd gone back into the fog, and she fought the urge to hug him.

From this spot on the pavement, she had a clear view out to the ocean and to the Boundary. There was no doubt it was closer now, or . . . bigger, somehow.

But it couldn't come to shore, could it? Eat the town, like Al said?

She looked back over at him, his dark hair plastered to his head, his football jersey damp. He'd gone into the fog before and lit the light, so they knew he could do it again. If the fog came as close as he said it would, Al could save them, right?

But, Bel wondered as she watched him smile at Nolie, would he? And if he didn't, could she be brave enough to do it instead?

CHAPTER 20

THE WIND WAS STRONG ENOUGH TO STING BEL'S EYES as she squinted out across the harbor. She and Mum had picked up some bacon rolls for breakfast on their way to open the shop and decided to stop and watch the boats for a bit. Even though there hadn't been any tourists interested in the early run today, Jaime and Bel's dad had decided to take the boat out anyway, letting Jaime get some more experience driving it instead of being the one to give the talk. The *Bonny Bel* looked small from this distance, like a toy, and she didn't like watching those steel-gray waves lift it up only to drop it back down.

"I hate that boat," her mum said from beside her, and Bel turned to look at her, surprised.

"You've never said that before."

Mum glanced down, her expression wry. "Well, I didn't want to hurt your brothers' feelings. Or your dad's, for that matter."

She put an arm around Bel's shoulders, squeezing her against her side, the soft wool of her jumper rubbing Bel's cheek. "But I can tell you these things, love," Mum continued. "Whole point of having a girl, really. Someone to tell my secrets to."

The reminder of secrets made Bel's stomach hurt, and she had to keep her eyes out at sea rather than turning to look left, toward the beach and the caves. What would her mum think if she told her about Al? About the lighthouse? Would she believe her, or think she was spending too much time with Nolie, letting fanciful ideas fill her head?

Stormy day like this, it would be wet down by the caves, the waves throwing their spray against the rock walls, the ceilings dripping. She hoped Al had the sense to stay in the attic today rather than go back down to the beach, but you never could tell with boys.

"I wonder what they take pictures of," Mum mused. "Those tourists who go out on the boat. Do they go home and show people big blobs of gray and say, 'Oh, aye, I went to Scotland, look at this!'"

Smiling, Bel nudged her. "They don't say 'aye' a'tall, Mum. And they probably just post the pictures on Facebook."

"Facebook," her mum sighed, like she couldn't even stand the idea of such a thing.

"It's an adventure," Bel reminded her. "Like all those people who go to Loch Ness. People like to think there might be a little magic in the world."

That made her mum glance down at her, a puzzled smile crinkling her face. "That doesn't sound like a very Bel McKissick thing to say."

"Nolie," Bel explained, and her mum nodded.

"Nolie."

She chafed one hand up and down Bel's arm, as though she were trying to keep her warm, and then said, "You're spending a lot of time with Nolie now."

"Not much else to do," Bel reminded her, but Mum was still watching her, eyes narrowed just a bit.

Then Mum shook her head, turning her gaze back out at the sea. "You're always the one to surprise me, my Bonny Bel," she said, and Bel looked up at her, confused.

"What do you mean?"

With a sigh, her mum rocked back on her heels a little. "Just that I always wonder with you. With Simon, I knew he'd never want to stay in Journey's End. With Jaime, I know he *will*. But you?"

Mum tilted her head down to smile at Bel. "You could go either way, I suppose."

Bel wasn't sure why, but those words made her feel warm and smiley, like she wanted to throw her arms around her mum's waist and hug her tight the way she used to when she was little. Bel had never been sure whether she wanted to stay or not—and figured she had a long time to work that out for herself—but it was nice, hearing her mum say she was "surprising." It seemed like a good thing to be.

"And as for you and Nolie," her mum went on, "so long as you stay put after sunset from now on, I suppose what you did isn't *so* bad."

Bel had been afraid she'd be grounded or even banned from hanging out with Nolie after the other night, but since she was hardly the first kid in Journey's End to take advantage of the long days in the summer, Mum had let her off with a warning.

"At least you came back at a sensible hour," she'd told Bel, and Bel knew her mum was remembering the time Jaime and Simon had gone to Wythe only to come in near two in the morning.

Once again, she was thankful for her disobedient big brothers. They made any trouble *she* got into seem mild in comparison.

Bel was just thinking she ought to go and see if she could find Nolie and Al when Mum let out a gasp.

Bel had been looking over her shoulder toward the village, not at the boat, but when she turned back, she could see the *Bonny Bel*'s white hull much closer to the fog than it had been before.

"Why are they so close?" her mum said in a low voice, and Bel had a feeling she was talking to herself more than to her. Still, she was wondering the same thing—was Jaime seeing how close he could get? Because now it seemed as though the fog was kissing the bow, gray sliding against white.

And then Bel realized what she was seeing.

"Mum!" she cried, tugging at her mother's sleeve. "It's not the boat getting closer to the fog, it's the fog—"

"Hush, Bel," her mum said sharply, like Bel saying the words would make what was happening more true somehow.

But it was clear as day to Bel that the fog was moving toward the boat, slinking and creeping over the water, reaching out long, misty tentacles. She couldn't hear anything from the *Bonny Bel* over the wind and waves; she could only *watch*.

Bel and her mum stood at the docks, Bel's fists clutched tight at her side, her mum's fingers pressed to her lips, watching. What else was there to do *but* watch? Suddenly Bel thought of all those other people in Journey's End, all those disappearances, and wondered if they'd also stood here on the docks, their hearts in their throats, watching as the Boundary moved closer to people they loved.

"Bel!"

She turned to see Nolie running to her, red hair streaming out behind her like a banner. She was in her purple boots as always, a bright green rain slicker pulled over her T-shirt and jeans. "What's happening?"

Nolie's dad was right behind her, a yellow plastic shopping bag in his hands. His glasses were dotted with mist, and he was squinting out at the Boundary. "Why did they get that close?" he asked.

Bel's mum didn't tear her eyes away from the sea, watching the fog roll over the front of the ship, the bow completely gone now. "It's not the boat; it's the Boundary," she said in a shaky voice. "Something's wrong."

That didn't seem like a strong enough way to put it when Bel was standing there, watching half the *Bonny Bel* vanish into the Boundary. All she could see were those pictures in the back of the shop, Jaime's and Dad's faces among them, and she turned panicked eyes to Nolie.

"We have to do something," she said, but she wasn't sure she was talking about what was unfolding in front of their eyes. For all that the idea of sending people—of sending *Al*—back into the fog horrified her, Bel now understood why the people in the village were willing to do it. She would do anything right now if it meant saving Jaime and Dad, anything that would keep the Boundary from slipping closer.

Farther down the docks, there was a flurry of activity. Another boat, one of the tour boats that wasn't as popular and couldn't hold as many people, was getting ready to go out. Bel and her mum hurried down that way, Nolie and her dad trailing behind.

"Dave!" Bel's mum called, and the man at the side of the boat, wearing a red toboggan cap, glanced up.

"Dinna fash, Fee," he said. "We'll go fetch them all back."

"It's just Jaime and Kenneth out there," Bel's mum told him, one hand pushing her hair back, her eyes wide and her voice tight. "There weren't any tourists this early."

Dave made a noise in the back of his throat. "Well, thank goodness for that, at least. Less to-do, then."

Bel thought there was plenty "to-do," seeing as how that was her dad and her brother out there, but she knew what Dave meant.

"You're not driving off into this, too, are you?" Nolie's dad asked, moving forward. He was right at the edge of the dock, pushing his glasses up with one knuckle. "It's too dangerous."

But Dave shook his head. "I'll get close as I can, have Jaime and Ken get aboard this one. Won't take a moment."

It was as good of a plan as Bel could think of, but when she looked back out at the sea, the fog seemed to have covered almost half the boat now, and Bel felt like there were bugs under her skin, everything feeling itchy and antsy and *hurry hurry hurry.*

"I'll go with you," Nolie's dad said, and Nolie's eyes went wide. "Dad," she started, clutching his arm, but he gave her a quick smile. In that moment, Bel could see how much Nolie looked like her dad. It was the same smile Nolie had given Bel dozens of times over the last week or so.

"I'll be fine, Nolie Mae," he told her. "But Dave here might need some help."

Dave's pursed lips said exactly how he felt about that.

"Not a place for you," he said, and Bel glanced around, realizing there was a small crowd forming. Several of them were looking at Nolie's dad with faces like stone, that same clamped, tight expression Dave was wearing, and Bel remembered how nervous Nolie's dad had seemed at the town meeting.

He was still nervous now, but he stood up a little straighter and said simply, "I want to help."

After a moment, Dave gave a quick nod and lifted a hand to help Nolie's dad clamber aboard.

The three of them—Nolie, Bel, and her mum— watched the *Caillte Cruise* putter out of the harbor and toward the *Bonny Bel,* the fog still covering half its deck even though Bel could see the water churned up by the engines. Her dad *had* to be putting it in reverse; he had to be.

Next to her, Nolie folded her arms. "It's going to be fine," she said, her shoulders pushed back, but her hands moving restlessly, tugging at her jacket, twisting the ring on her pinkie.

Bel could only nod, her heart in her throat, that *hurry* feeling making her wiggle her fingers as though that would make Dave's boat go faster. Fifteen minutes. It took the *Bonny Bel* fifteen minutes to reach the Boundary, and that was only because they went so slowly, drawing out the trip as best they could. Dave was going faster; he'd be there quicker.

And sure enough, the *Caillte Cruise* was pulling up just behind the *Bonny Bel* a little over five minutes later, but that waiting felt like forever to Bel.

"It's okay," Nolie said, reaching out to hold Bel's hand. They twined their fingers together like the knots Bel's dad had taught her to make, like the ropes that were forever scraping Jaime's palms because he never wore his gloves.

Tears stung Bel's eyes, but she took deep breaths. "They're there now," she said, talking to herself like Mum had earlier. Her mum had moved farther down the docks, still watching, one arm wrapped around her middle.

"They're there," Nolie echoed, and Bel gave her hand

a squeeze. Any minute now, people would be moving off the *Bonny Bel* and onto the *Caillte Cruise*. Any minute—

And then, as she watched, the fog suddenly surged forward, like a horse hearing a starting pistol, and rolled over not just the *Bonny Bel*, but the *Caillte Cruise* as well, and both boats vanished into the gray.

FROM "THE SAD TALE OF CAIT MCINNISH,"
CHAPTER 13,
Legends of the North

THE SKY GREW DARKER, AND THE FOG THAT SLUNK low across the ground of the lighthouse and its island grew thicker. A small part of Cait wished she hadn't put out the lighthouse's flame, leaving her alone in the darkness, but then she remembered that it was not *her* fault she was cast adrift in this place.

They had left her here to disappear so they wouldn't have to watch her die. This village, this *home*, wanted her gone from their sight.

Cait sat and the boat rocked and the fog grew and the dark that had curled around her heart blotted out all fear, all sadness, until everything was anger.

Anger and fog.

Cait, the girl who did not believe in magic or fairy stories, looked at the coastline of her village in the distance and willed the fog rising up around her to grow thicker still, to reach grasping fingers toward the mainland.

Let it grow, she thought. *Let it reach. Let it take. Until my father's light is lit again, let this fog consume everyone and every-thing in its path. Let their daughters and sons disappear as they wished me to do.*

And so the village on the edge of the Caillte Sea be-came a cursed place with a fog that slid in from the sea, thick and gray.

When the first ship foundered against the rocks, the laird sent a boat of his men to light the lighthouse.

They never returned.

He sent a second boat, a third, and when neither of them returned either, the whispers began. Whispers that the witch had lived, perhaps was making the island her home, and was sending this fog as a punishment.

The laird listened to none of it until the fog crept over the harbor of the village, taking an entire ship and the harbormaster with it.

It was then that panic began to inch through the vil-lage as surely as the fog had. When it slid in far enough to take the house nearest the sea, panic became terror, and all might have been lost had it not been for the laird's daughter.

Older than poor, doomed Rabbie, Margaret had loved her brother, but she had counted Cait a friend, and she'd hoped that friendship might let her pass through the fog unharmed.

Perhaps it had. After Margaret went, the light was lit, and the fog slid back to surround the rocky outcrop where the lighthouse stood. The village was safe, and if young Margaret never returned from her journey, the laird and the villagers alike counted it a fair price to pay.

And so the cursed village of Journey's End crouched by the Caillte Sea and held its breath, praying the light would never go out again.

CHAPTER 21

NOLIE WATCHED THE FOG EAT BOTH OF THE BOATS IN front of her, and for what felt like forever, could only stare at the giant . . . *cloud* where the boats had been.

Next to her, Bel gave a choked cry, and Bel's mum dropped a hand to Bel's shoulder, her own face gray, lips pressed tightly together.

"They'll come back," Nolie heard herself say. "They . . . they have to, they can't just . . ."

Except they could. People disappeared in Journey's End all the time, taken by that same fog she'd just watched swallow two boats. Suddenly Nolie thought she might throw up.

"It's all right," Bel's mum said, her voice firm even though her face was still roughly the same color as that fog. "It's all right," she repeated.

It very clearly was not all right. There was already a hive of activity down at the harbor. Watching men in sweaters and jeans walk down to the edge of the pier, their hands shading their eyes as they peered out at the Boundary, Nolie was reminded of when there were power outages back home in Georgia. There was that same feeling of everybody wanting to see what was going on.

She almost said all of that to Bel and her mum, but the words seemed stuck in her throat as she kept staring out at the sea. Any minute now, the boats would reappear. They'd *have* to.

But they stood there for what felt like forever, and there was nothing. Just the fog on the water, rolling and almost pulsing, and Nolie definitely thought she was going to throw up now.

"Stop!" she heard Bel's mum call out, and for a second, she thought it was an order not to cry. But when she looked up, Bel's mum was waving her arms over her head at the men approaching the harbor, men who were clearly heading toward their own boats.

"Don't!" she yelled again, and then jogged off toward them. She was too far away for Nolie or Bel to hear what she was saying, but they both watched her shake her head as she spoke to one of the men, a dark-haired guy in an olive-green jacket. Both of them kept gesturing out at the Boundary, their faces red from more than just the wind.

"Mum is right," Bel said softly, her fingers flexing against Nolie's. "She's telling them not to go. And they shouldn't. They'll just get sucked in, too."

Nolie gave a violent shiver that had nothing to do with the cold. "Like a horror movie," she said, her stomach still rolling. "Everyone goes looking for the people who've disappeared, and then *they* disappear."

Bel didn't reply, but her grip got tighter.

Nolie watched Bel's mum argue with the man in the jacket, wondering what the heck they could do now. This was *big*. Really big. If her dad didn't come back, would they call her mom back in Georgia? Should she call her *now*? And say what? "Hi, Mom, this trip to Scotland hasn't gone so well, mostly because Dad disappeared in a magical fog bank."

"What are we going to do?" she heard herself say, her voice sounding high and thin to her own ears. The more she stared at the sea, the stranger—and worse—she felt, like everything inside of her was shaking. People *didn't* come back from the Boundary. That was its whole *deal*.

"Al," Bel said, giving Nolie's hand another squeeze. "We have Al, and that . . . has to mean this time is different, right?"

Nolie looked over at Bel. "Al," she repeated, and then nodded quickly. "Yeah, exactly. We can . . . we can fix this."

She didn't know how, but the words made her feel better at least, and Nolie lifted her head, her eyes searching out Albert's dark hair or Nessie hat, but there was no sign of him.

Bel's mum was making her way back to them now, scrubbing a hand over her hair. As she got closer, she turned toward Nolie, and Nolie noticed again just how much Bel's mum looked like Bel, with her little nose and bright hazel eyes.

"Nolie," she said, "is anyone else at the Institute right now?"

It was such an unexpected question that Nolie could only shake her head, confused. "N-no," she managed to say, thinking back to a talk she and her dad had just had on their way into the village to pick up breakfast. "Dr. Burkhart is in Inverness for the next two days. It's just Dad right now. Or it . . . it was . . ." Her voice seemed to disappear in her suddenly tightening throat, and she felt Bel squeeze her hand again, their fingers still tightly interlocked.

Bel's mum gave a quick nod. "All right," she said. "You can stay with us until this all gets sorted out, and . . ." Nolie could see Mrs. McKissick suck in a deep breath as she glanced back out at the harbor, then again to her. "I suspect you'll be wanting to call your mum."

Nolie *did* want to call her mom. A lot. But she also knew that if she did, she wouldn't be able to lie to her about what was happening out here. Nolie had always been a terrible liar, never really *needing* to lie about anything. And if she told Mom what had happened . . .

Still, she shook her head no, and Bel's mum gave her a tight, forced smile in reply.

"They'll probably be back soon anyway," Mrs. McKissick said. "Just . . . sailed into the fog a bit, and she'll chug right back out again. We're all going to feel right silly in a few minutes, I'd reckon."

Nolie really hoped that was true, but they stood there for nearly an hour, and nothing happened. And the longer they waited, the more Nolie thought about her dad, about how much she'd missed him just over these past six months. What if she never saw him again at all?

After a long, long while, Bel's mum looked back at the two of them and said, "I have to get Jack from nursery. Bel, can you go close up the shop? And then we'll . . ."

She didn't bother finishing the sentence, and Nolie didn't really blame her. What was there to say, after all? We'll figure out some way to save everyone from the fog that just ate two boats right in front of our faces?

She headed off toward the little daycare Jack went to, and Nolie and Bel headed for the shop, both of them lost in their own thoughts.

When they opened the door, Nolie was surprised to see Albert peeking out from behind the rack of silly hats.

"How did you get in here?" Nolie asked, and Albert shrugged, pointing at the door.

"It was open," he said, "and I wanted a new pair of

trousers." Nolie noticed that he was still wearing the jersey Bel had given him, but now he wore black track pants with an outline of Scotland in white down one leg. "I'll pay you back for them," he told Bel, who just waved a hand at him.

"Are you both all right?" he asked, stepping out into the store. "I saw what happened," he continued, nodding at the window and the Boundary beyond. "I wanted to go out, but—"

"No," Bel said quickly. "It's better that you didn't." Then she glanced around, and gestured both Nolie and Al to the back of the store and into the big storage room where all the extra stuff was kept.

While the front of the store was cozy and lamp-lit, this room had concrete floors, lots of metal shelving, and fluorescent lights. Nolie grimaced as she looked for a place to sit.

Albert dumped a crate of stuffed sheep onto the floor, flipping it over so he could sit on it, and while Nolie wanted to tell him to be nicer to Sir Woolington's siblings, she just gathered them up in her arms and put them on a shelf behind her.

Bel was still standing in the middle of the room, chewing on her thumbnail, her eyes focused somewhere just over Nolie's shoulder.

Nolie didn't think she was actually *looking* at anything, though.

It was Albert who spoke first. "D'ye see now?" he asked. "Why they kept it secret? It'll start up here, too, just like it did in my time. They'll send a few more boats, and when those go missing and the fog comes closer, they'll start talking about the legends. About the lighthouse."

"Then what?" Nolie asked, her sneakers squeaking on the floor. "Even if someone did go out there to light it, that person would get stuck, too. Like you did, all . . . preserved, like a fossil."

"S'pose fossil is better than zombie," Albert muttered.

Ignoring that, Nolie folded her arms and said, "Wait. But when you lit the light, did those people who'd gone missing come *back*?"

"He wouldn't know," Bel interjected. "He was being a fossil."

"Oh, right," Nolie mused, and from his place on the crate, Albert threw up his hands.

"I wasna a *fossil*," he said, but then his expression changed.

"They could have," he said. "They *might* have. That tearoom you took me to. I told you there'd been a building there, but the fog took it. I can't be sure that's the same building, but it . . . it could be?"

"But the pictures," Bel countered, chewing on her thumbnail. "On the back wall of the shop. Those people were always missing. They didn't come back."

"Or they did, and the village never talked about it," Nolie answered, her heart pounding faster now. "You heard Albert; they've always kept things to do with the Boundary a secret. Maybe he lit that light back in 1918, and everything just . . . went back to how it was, but no one talked about it."

"So what?" Bel asked, dropping her hand. "You think if we lit the light, we could get our dads out?"

It was almost too scary to hope, but Nolie nodded anyway. "I think we could."

And then Bel sighed, crossing her arms. "In that case," she said, "I think there's something we need to do."

CHAPTER 22

"Is this the best font to say 'We're not crazy, Please Listen to Us'?"

Bel leaned over Nolie's shoulder, looking at the computer screen. They were at the Institute, using Nolie's dad's laptop. Al sat at the other computer, the big desktop one, playing solitaire.

"I'm not sure there is a font for that, Nolie," Bel told her, "but I like this one."

The words were big and black and serious. Town Meeting, they proclaimed, At Town Hall, Tonight, 6:00.

The idea was that no one would know who called the meeting, so they might actually get people to show up. It was also why they wanted the meeting to be so soon— the less time people had to ask who might be calling this, the better.

"Brilliant!" Al enthused from his corner, and Nolie looked over her shoulder at him.

"You like the font?" she asked, and Al turned, blinking.

"The what? I just won a wee card game on this box," he explained, waving his hand on the screen. "What else can I do on here?"

Nolie turned back to her flyer. "Al, we do not have time to get into the internet with you right now, so please just . . . stay there with the card game, okay?"

Al took that well enough, shrugging and opening another game of solitaire.

"Should we say what the meeting is about?" Nolie asked Bel.

Taking a seat next to Nolie at the long table, Bel shook her head. "They'll know, I'd think. What else is there to talk about besides what happened today?"

Nolie highlighted the time of the meeting, making it bigger and turning it yellow before shaking her head and making the words black again. "All kinds of things," she said before hitting print. "How great the stuffed sheep in your shop are, Al's record at *Dance Your Pants Off* . . ."

It was typical Nolie, making a joke whenever she could, but Bel could tell her heart wasn't really in it. She was still looking at the screen, tapping the knuckle of one finger against her mouth, her knee bouncing underneath the table. And Bel hadn't missed the way Nolie had blinked back tears when they'd come into the Institute . . . the big house had seemed so empty and quiet.

Not that Bel was feeling much better. But this, having a plan, *doing* something, helped. The printer began spitting out copies of the flyer, and Bel looked over at the machine, taking a deep breath. It wasn't that she thought this was a bad idea, exactly, but she wasn't sure how her mum was going to react. Still, if there was a chance they could work out how to save their dads and Jaime, then it was worth the risk. No one else in the town knew what to do, but they did. They had Al.

The smell of hot ink filled the little room as more and more flyers shot out of the printer. Bel went to stand beside Nolie, crossing her arms over her chest. "How many of those are you printing?" she asked, and now it was Nolie's turn to shrug.

"Two hundred? Figure that'll give us enough to really paper the town."

Eyes widening, Bel looked at the growing stack of flyers and nodded. "Yeah, that'll . . . that'll do it, all right."

"Ah!" Al suddenly cried from behind them, and they both turned to see him scooting back from the computer. "Nolie, I've done something!"

There was a graphic on the screen of a phone wiggling back and forth, and with a hiss, Nolie pushed off from her table, sending her rolling chair crashing into Al's desk. "My mom," she said.

"Are you going to answer it?" Bel asked, and Nolie glanced over at her.

"I have to. If I don't, she'll be worried and try to call Dad."

Al scooted back as Nolie clicked something, and then a square appeared on the screen, showing a woman with blond hair and Nolie's smile. She was in a bright white kitchen, cheerful yellow curtains hung over a sink behind her, and Bel realized it must still be really early in Georgia.

"Noles?" Nolie's mom asked, and Nolie leaned over, waving at the little camera at the top of the computer monitor.

"Hi, Mom!" she said, a little too loudly, and the woman on the screen immediately frowned.

"What's wrong?" she asked, and Nolie sighed, shifting so that her chair was closer to the screen.

"Nothing!" she insisted, but when she started drumming her fingers on the desk, Bel quietly reached over and covered them, just out of sight of the camera. Al was still sitting off to the side, his mouth hanging open.

"That's a thing you can do on these, too?" he whispered. "Talk to people *through the screen?*"

Nolie waved a hand at him under the desk, hoping her mom didn't see. "Just, you know, hanging out. Doing Scottish things."

Nolie's mom didn't seem convinced. She had her lips pressed in a tight line and her eyes scanning her own screen, like if she could just see through it, she'd see whatever was going on with her daughter.

"Are you by yourself?" she asked, and Nolie shook her head, gesturing for Bel to come into view.

"No, I'm hanging out with friends, see? This is Bel and this"—Nolie reached over, dragging Al closer—"is Albert, and um, they're my friends. My new Scottish friends."

Bel and Al both waved at the camera, and Nolie's mom settled back, relieved. "Oh, good! What are the three of you up to?"

Bel tried not to chew on her fingernails, and Al was already slinking back out of the shot, but Nolie just said, "Oh, you know, calling a town meeting to talk about how we need to go light a magical lighthouse."

Biting back a squeak, Bel stood very still, just staring at the computer and wondering if Nolie had lost her mind with all this stress. But Nolie's mom just laughed. She laughed the same way Nolie did, big and loud, showing lots of teeth.

"Well, I certainly don't want to keep you from that," she said. "But I missed your face. Have you sent me a letter?"

"I sent three yesterday," Nolie said, reaching out to tap the screen. "And I miss your face, too."

"And you got the package I sent? With the book you wanted?"

Nolie's shoulders went up a little bit and she ducked her head, not looking at Bel or Al. Bel wondered what *that* was about.

"Yup, got it, thanks," Nolie said quickly, and her mom smiled.

"You three be good, okay?" Nolie's mom said, and Bel gave another wave and a nod. "We will!" she said, striving for some of Nolie's brightness.

"We will," Al echoed, still far out of the camera's sight.

Nolie's mom leaned a little closer. "And call me back tonight or tomorrow, okay? Alone? I have some questions." She gave a broad wink at that, and Nolie groaned, the tips of her ears turning pink.

Nolie waved a hand and said, "Okay, okay, I love you, Embarrassing Mom."

"I love you, Embarrassed Daughter," her mom replied, and then, after blowing Nolie a kiss, she was gone.

Nolie took a deep breath, leaning back in her chair, hands on top of her head.

"Why did you do that?" Bel asked. "Tell her the truth?"

Nolie sat up, hands dropping heavily into her lap. "I can't lie to my mom. I'm terrible at it. So I figured I would just tell the truth, see if that worked out. And it did, so yay."

The printer was quiet now, all their flyers printed, and Bel went to gather them as Nolie rose from her chair. Al was still giving the computer a longing look, and Nolie snapped her fingers at him.

"Flyers and meeting now, solitaire later," she promised. And then she snapped her fingers again, looking up. "Ooh! Hold on!" she said, and took off down the hall.

Bel shook her head, picking up the flyers and handing some of them to Al. "I don't know if this will work," she confessed, and he took the papers, jaw clenched.

"You should let me tell them," he said, and Bel shook her head, fingers tightening around her own stack of flyers.

"Al, we talked about this. The less weird we can make this seem, the more chance they have of listening to us. We just need to tell them about the light, not ... not you. Just in case."

"What is it you think they'll do to me?" Al asked, leaning one hip against the table. "Take me to a laboratory, cut me up?"

"Worse," Nolie said, coming back into the room, a backpack slung over one shoulder. "Put you on reality TV. Are we ready?"

Bel nodded, heading for the door. "We have to move quickly," she told the other two over her shoulder. "Get as many up as we can, as fast as we can."

With that, she flung open the front door of the Institute, only to find herself running smack into someone.

"Oh!" Bel cried, staggering back.

And then she realized who it was standing there.

CHAPTER 23

"LESLIE," BEL SAID, STUNNED, AND LESLIE WIGGLED HER fingers, almost like a wave.

"Hi," she said. "I'm sorry, I just . . . I heard what happened, and I thought you might be up here with—" Her gaze drifted over Bel's shoulder to where Nolie stood, still holding her backpack, Al just behind her with his stack of flyers.

"I'm sorry," Leslie said again, meeting Bel's eyes for what felt like the first time in forever. And Bel thought she might be apologizing for more than what had happened with the boats.

"Okay," Bel replied, because she didn't know what else to say. Then she cleared her throat and handed Leslie some of the flyers. "Do you want to . . . do you want to help us put these up around town?"

Leslie nodded quickly, not even really looking at the flyers, her shoulders sagging a little. "Oh, sure," she said brightly, even as Nolie narrowed her eyes at her.

"You're really going to help, right? Not just *say* you're going to help, then throw our flyers in the trash, or something?"

Leslie looked up, tugging her bottom lip between her teeth. "I wouldn't do that," she said softly, and from behind Nolie, Al gave what sounded like a snort.

"Even if Alice told you to?" Bel asked softly, and Leslie met her gaze.

"Even then," she said.

Bel thought for a moment. Leslie had apologized about the prank with Maggie, and maybe this was her way of trying to make up for *all* of it, not just the prank.

Rocking forward on the balls of her feet, Leslie looked at the flyers in Bel's hands. "What's this all about?" she asked.

Even if Bel was willing to trust Leslie with the flyers, she still wasn't ready to trust her with much of the truth. No need getting into *why* they had called this meeting.

Taking a deep breath, Bel thrust a handful of flyers into Leslie's arms. "Don't worry about that," she said at last. "Put these up. Wherever you think people will see them."

Leslie's cheeks turned pink, but she smiled, nodding quickly, and the four of them set off down toward the village.

The hall was full before six, people milling about, voices buzzing. Bel had heard at least five different people wonder aloud who had called the meeting, and as she stood next to the wall with Nolie, she tried not to look as nervous as she felt.

"Stop chewing your fingernails," Nolie said in a low voice, and Bel dropped her hand, realizing she clearly wasn't looking relaxed.

Journey's End town hall was hardly ever used anymore, although Cara McLendon's older sister had held her wedding reception there the year before. That's what it was mostly used for now—get-togethers, the occasional party. It was just a big, old building with exactly one big room, although at some point in the 1980s, someone had installed a loo. Bel had actually never been in the building before tonight.

They'd agreed that Al would wait outside, and Bel glanced toward the window, wondering where he might have hidden himself. But as she did, she met eyes with her mum, walking in with Jack perched on one hip.

Mum waved her over, and Bel obeyed, her feet dragging just a little bit. "There you are," she said. "What have you been up to all day?"

But before Bel could answer, there was a scraping sound as Nolie dragged a chair to the front of the room.

Climbing up on that chair, Nolie stuck her fingers in her mouth, blowing out an ear-piercing whistle that had Bel wincing.

Even Nolie looked a little abashed at how loud it was, her shoulders rising to her ears, but the room *had* fallen quiet, a sea of faces now turned toward Nolie.

"Um," Nolie began. "Thank you all for coming. We'd like to begin now."

There was silence for a few heartbeats, and then the voices all started up again as everyone realized just *who* had called this meeting.

Bel's mum stepped forward, Jack still in her arms, and Bel fought the urge to wring her hands.

"Girls," she said firmly. "What is this about?"

"We're not wasting anyone's time, Mrs. McKissick," Nolie said quickly, still standing on the chair. "I promise. But we think we know how to help get our dads and Jaime back, and we wanted to talk to the town about it."

At that, Mum's expression softened, the corners of her mouth turning down slightly. "Oh, love," she said to Bel. "I know you're worried—we all are. But once the fog clears a bit—"

"It's not going to clear," Bel said, her voice stronger than she would've thought, given how nervous she was. "We have to go get them, Mum."

Now her mum's mouth was trembling slightly. "Bel," she began, but Nolie was already stepping down from the chair, offering it to Bel.

Bel stepped up, her trainers squeaking a little, and as she faced all the people who had come out to the meeting, she couldn't help but tug her sleeves over her fingers. "It's the lighthouse," she said, her voice carrying in the quiet room. "When the light isn't lit, the fog comes closer and things—*people*—disappear. Someone has to light the light to make the fog go away."

No one said anything to that, and as Bel looked out, she realized everyone was watching her with similar expressions of pity. They felt *sorry* for her, poor little girl, so desperate to get her dad and brother back that she'd rely on an old story.

And seeing all those people feeling sorry for her just made Bel angry. "It's true," she said, a little louder. "And it's happened before. In 1918."

She and Nolie had talked about this, what exactly to say at the meeting. Neither of them wanted to tell people about Al, but they needed everyone to understand that they knew what they were talking about.

"The fog came closer, and Albert MacLeish lit the lamp. It made the fog go back to the island and stop coming near the shore. So that's . . . that's what we have to do now."

From the back of the room, Leslie's mum stood up. Like Leslie, she had dark hair, although hers was cut short. "Bel, it's a good story, love, it is, but why in heaven's name would lighting a lamp make a bit of difference about the Boundary?"

"I might have an idea?" Nolie said, stepping forward, her backpack in her hands. "About why this happened."

And then, to Bel's horror, she pulled out a book called *Legends of the North.* "Y'all don't sell this here in town, but my—my mom sent it to me, and there's a story—"

She had just opened the book when Bel's mum stepped forward, gently laying a hand on her shoulder. "Nolie," she said. "We're all worried and upset, but fairy stories aren't going to help us now."

Nolie's ears and cheeks were pink, but she stood up a little straighter. "It's not a fairy story," she said, "It's *history*, and I think it might—"

"The girls are right."

Everyone in the hall turned to see Maggie McLeod standing in the doorway. The first time Bel had seen her up close, at her house, she'd thought Maggie was older than she'd ever guessed, but looking at her now, standing up so straight and tall, she couldn't be sure.

"It's the lighthouse," she said. "It must be lit to hold back the fog."

There was silence in the room for a moment, then the

soft shushing noise of people fidgeting where they stood. Next to Bel, Nolie was pressed tight against her side, stretching up on her tiptoes for a better look.

After a moment, Bel's mum cleared her throat. "Maggie," she said, in that same tone she'd used to talk to Nolie. "I'm sure there are all sorts of legends about this place, but—" She broke off with a disbelieving and almost embarrassed laugh. "It doesn't seem like lighting a lighthouse that's over five hundred years old is the solution. What we need is to send out a few boats—"

"Those boats will vanish," Maggie said. "As all the boats have when this happened before. The only thing that will save Journey's End is for someone to row to that island and light that light. The person you send will never return."

Bel couldn't help but glance behind her at the window, where she could just make out the top of Al's dark head as he crouched outside, listening. Nolie looked over at her, too, eyebrows raised.

And then, to Bel's shock, she realized Maggie was looking at her, too. "Well," the old woman amended, "they won't return for some time, at least."

Bel stood there, frozen and staring at Maggie. She knew. She had to. Even from this distance, Bel thought she could almost make out a twinkle in Maggie's eye as she said that, and then Maggie was looking back at Mum.

"You want to save this town and your loved ones, light the light, and the fog will recede. What you've lost will be returned. It's the only way."

And then, apparently having said all she intended to say, Maggie turned and walked out the door.

CHAPTER 24

THERE WAS SILENCE AFTER MAGGIE LEFT, AND THEN, LIKE a gust of wind blowing through the room, the talk started up again, voices hushed but urgent.

At her place near the window, Bel's mum was frowning, arms folded so tightly that her hands were cupped around her elbows, and Nolie saw her nodding at something that Leslie's mum was saying.

Nolie looked at Bel and nodded at the door.

They stepped out of the hall, and into the damp, cool evening. Albert walked over from his hiding place behind the fountain, glancing around nervously.

"What happened?" he asked, and Nolie shook her head, looking off in the direction of Maggie's house.

But before she could answer him, Bel faced her. "You couldn't have told me about the book?"

Surprised, Nolie widened her eyes. "That book had good stuff in it!" she argued. "There's this legend about a girl sent off in a boat, and while it doesn't *say* it happened in Journey's End, it *could* have. I was just . . ."

Suddenly feeling defeated, Nolie lifted her arms and then let them drop. "I was trying to help."

They were all quiet, Albert shifting his weight, looking between them, and Nolie shoved her hands in her pockets, turning to him.

"Maggie told them," she said. "About the lighthouse and the curse, and how people have to go light it, but then they don't come back."

Albert's dark brows shot up on his forehead. "And what did everyone say?"

Nolie looked over at Bel. She was wearing her yellow jacket tonight, and had it fastened up to her chin. Her blond hair whipped around her face as she sighed and said, "About what you'd think. That it was nonsense and a fairy story, and all of that."

Albert shoved his hands in his pockets, shoulders rolling. "So what do we do now?"

"We follow her, obviously," Nolie replied, and began marching in the general direction of Maggie's house, her hands clenched into fists.

To her left, she could see the Boundary rising up off the water. When she'd first come to Journey's End, it had seemed weird and maybe a little mysterious, but nothing all that sinister. But now her *dad* was out in that thing, and Bel's dad and brother, too.

"Maggie is clearly the answer," she told Bel and Albert over the rising wind. Under her feet, the cobblestone streets in the city center were slippery, and she was glad she was wearing her wellies.

Her purple wellies with the flowers on them. The ones her dad bought for her.

Swallowing down the sudden lump in her throat, Nolie added, "If the people in the village won't listen to her, fine. *We* will."

"The last time we went up there, she thought we were playing a prank on her," Albert reminded Nolie, moving fast to keep up with her. Bel was a few steps behind, shooting glances at the town hall over her shoulder every few seconds. "She isn't going to want to help us."

"She is once we tell her about you," Nolie said, and Albert came skidding to such a sudden stop that Bel nearly ran into him.

"About me? How I came back?"

"No, about your deep love for ice cream cones," Nolie answered, rolling her eyes. "Of *course* about how you lit the light and came back. If she knows the stories, she'll know what to do. She'll believe us. Besides, I think she recognized you that night we went up there."

Albert's shoulders rose. "Probably from my picture in Bel's shop," he reminded Nolie. "What if she tells Bel's mum about me, or calls the police? Where will we be then, Nolie?"

It was a good point, and one Nolie didn't really like thinking about all that much. She just wanted to save her dad and Bel's family, too, and here was Maggie, maybe having an answer. To Nolie's mind, it seemed like a risk worth taking, but when she turned to Bel, she could see her friend wasn't sold, either. Her hands had once again disappeared into the sleeves of her jacket, and she was chewing her lower lip, still looking back toward the town hall.

"We have to do something," Nolie said, keeping her voice a little lower. She could feel that tight sensation in her throat again, and was suddenly afraid she was going to cry. "You saw that meeting tonight, Bel. No one knows what to do because this is all too weird and too scary, and no one wants to admit that there might be something honestly freaky about all of it. They're going to have meetings and wonder and worry until the fog is at the village, and by then it might be too late."

Overhead, the clouds were getting thicker, almost the same gray as the Boundary, and Nolie felt like the whole world might be turning that color. Like they were all trapped inside a snow globe, but instead of glitter and water, they were about to be surrounded by a thick fog. Maybe forever.

Finally, Bel gave a firm nod. "You're right," she said, and Nolie let out a long breath. "We have to at least try. If she won't talk to us, or panics about Al, we'll . . . just have to cross that bridge when we come to it."

"I've never heard anyone say it that way before," Albert muttered, but after a pause, he fell in step behind them.

They wound their way up from Journey's End to the tall green hills around the village, just like they had the other night. It was earlier this time, but thanks to all the clouds, the day was darker and the wind coming off the ocean felt particularly cold. Was that the Boundary, too? Nolie wondered. Did it feel cold? Was her dad in there even now with Bel's dad and brother, shivering on that boat, surrounded by all that rolling fog?

The idea of it made her stomach hurt, and she turned to look at Albert. He still had his hands in his pockets, his head bent. "What do you remember?" she asked him. "About the fog, specifically. Was it cold in there, were you scared . . . ?"

Albert paused, lifting his head. His cheeks were red from the wind, his mouth pursed slightly as he thought. Once again, Nolie couldn't get over how . . . normal he was starting to look. Like he belonged in their time after all.

"Aye, it was cold," he said at last. "But not an unnatural cold. Just . . . the regular sort, I s'pose. It's hard to remember now."

"What do you mean?" Bel asked. She'd fished a hair elastic out of her pocket now, and was trying to pull her hair back into a stubby little ponytail.

Albert shrugged, ducking his head again. "Just that once I got there, it was like the fog was in my mind itself. It was hard to think, hard to remember why I was there. And I can barely remember leaving. Just that one second I was on the shore, and the next, I was in my boat."

"And you don't remember rowing around for a long time, either, right?" Nolie asked. "Even though you were there for, like, a hundred years."

Albert nodded. "Only felt like a wee bit to me."

"That makes sense," Bel said, scuffing her boot along a loose stone on the path. "There's something magic about the fog, so the fog doing magic on your brain makes sense."

Nolie stopped, looking at her friend with wide eyes. "Um, Bel, did you just admit that *magic is afoot?*"

Bel scrunched up her face. "I did. I don't like that I did, but I did." She gave another look back to the village. "Or maybe it's just that right now, some magic would be nice."

Nolie understood that.

They started walking again, Nolie's legs burning the

farther uphill they went. Once they were at the top of the hill, the ruined castle clear in the distance, all three of them stopped and stared.

"Why did we ever take boats out to it?" Bel said. "How *didn't* that seem terrifying?"

"I thought the same thing the morning it took my brother," Al added. "That it seemed so stupid not to see how dangerous it was."

Almost like it could hear them, the Boundary seemed to bulge out, sliding across the gray waters of the Caillte Sea, churning like something in a cauldron.

"It's not fog. It's a curse."

The three of them turned around to see Maggie standing there, her gray hair blowing around her face, her hands on her hips. "But then, I think the three of you have that figured out."

CHAPTER 25

MAGGIE'S HOUSE DIDN'T SEEM SO SPOOKY AS THEY approached it this time, but maybe that's because it wasn't dark yet. Or maybe, Bel decided as she trudged through the grass toward the front steps, it was because Maggie was with them now, and there wouldn't be any knocking on doors, any trying to explain what was going on.

The lights were on inside, spilling out the front windows, and as Maggie opened the front door, she glanced over her shoulder at Bel, Nolie, and Al.

"Wipe your feet."

They obeyed as Maggie went on into the foyer, and Nolie leaned close to Bel. "What do you think it'll be like inside there?" she whispered.

"Maybe like the attic at the Institute?" Bel replied.

Nolie nodded. "Yup. Lots of paintings, some plants. Really old furniture."

Their shoes cleaned, the trio stepped into Maggie's

foyer. It was a lot like Bel had expected, all warm, polished wood, the scent of tea and candles in the air, and one wall dominated by a giant tapestry of a girl sitting in a forest, a unicorn at her feet.

But when they followed Maggie farther down the hall, the house . . . changed.

They walked into what had probably once been the front parlor of the house, back when people had used parlors. It was a cozy room, the walls wood-paneled and the ceiling low with heavy wooden beams running across it, and big windows facing the loch behind the house, but there was also a huge flat-screen TV affixed to one wall, and while the deep brown sofa looked expensive and comfortable, it also seemed pretty modern to Bel. In fact, the whole room seemed to be filled with the latest model of everything. A tablet, phone, and laptop computer were charging on a table, and big, beautiful photographs of cities at night lined the walls.

"Whoa," Nolie said under her breath, and Al stood transfixed, frowning at the giant television.

Glancing around, Maggie seemed to notice her surroundings for the first time. "What?" she asked them. "You think I'm too old for technology?"

"It's not that," Bel hurried to say, but Nolie just snorted.

"It's *exactly* that," she countered, and then added, "This room is really weird. No offense."

Bel elbowed Nolie, but Maggie smiled. "I'll give you that. Can I make you some tea?"

"Yes, please," Bel answered, only to have Nolie nudge her this time.

"Maybe that's not a good idea," she whispered, her gaze darting to Maggie's back as the older lady headed into the adjoining kitchen. "You know, eating or drinking things in the house of a . . . a . . ."

She trailed off, and Bel wasn't sure if it was because Nolie just didn't want to say what she thought Maggie was, or because she didn't know.

Maggie turned again, smiling at all three of them. "A witch? Is that what you wanted to say, lass?"

Nolie stared at Maggie for a moment. "If I say yes, are you going to eat me?" she asked, and Maggie laughed.

"No, yer a mite too bony for me." With that, she winked and disappeared into the kitchen, leaving the three of them to stand around her living room, unsure of what to do next.

Luckily, it didn't take Maggie long to make the tea, and she came back with a full tray only a few minutes later, nodding for the three of them to sit.

Bel lowered herself onto the leather sofa and Nolie and Al squeezed in on either side.

Maggie bowed her head, fussing with the tea, but Bel thought she was smiling again. "Here," she said, handing them their cups. Steam rose from the mugs, smelling sweet and lemony. The mug warmed Bel's hands, and she wrapped her fingers around it as she blew on its surface.

Al took a sip of his while Nolie was still staring at the cup like she didn't quite trust it. Maggie, sitting in the wingback chair across from the sofa, just leaned back and looked at them.

"Go ahead," she said after a moment. "Ask what it is you came here to ask."

"How did you know about the fog?" Nolie blurted, and Bel cut her a look. It might have been nice to ease into things a bit.

But Maggie didn't seem offended. She shrugged, sipping her own tea. "Because I was here when it was first conjured up," she said, and for a moment, there was silence in the room.

Bel found her voice first. "'Conjured'?" she echoed, and Maggie nodded. She set her mug back on the low table in front of her.

"Aye. There was no fog a'tall in Journey's End until Cait McInnish was sent onto the Caillte Sea in 1553."

Another moment of silence in the room as all three of them took that in.

"1553," Nolie said slowly. "And you were . . . there."

Maggie nodded, and Bel studied her face. She was old, there was no doubt of that. Her hair was completely silver, and when she picked up her tea again, Bel could see how bony her fingers were. So old, definitely, but nearly five hundred years old?

"Surely you can't be surprised," Maggie said, leaning back in her chair. Outside, the wind had picked up again, pushing clouds across the sky and sending shafts of sunlight through the big window that overlooked the loch. "Not with this one here." She nodded at Al, who was still sitting stiffly next to Bel.

"In the year of our Lord, 1553, my brother Rabbie fell from a window," Maggie continued, "and in his grief, my father, the laird, blamed Rabbie's nanny, Cait. Her punishment was to be put in a boat and set adrift in the Caillte Sea."

Next to Bel, Nolie sucked in a breath. "That was the story!" she said, bumping Bel with her elbow. And then the excitement faded from her face. "That's intense," she said, and Bel remembered how shaky Nolie had been on the *Bonny Bel* that one afternoon. Being left at sea would be a nightmare for anyone, but it was no surprise that Nolie would find it especially horrific.

"That's a word for it," Maggie agreed. "And then, after Cait, the fog came. Right out from the wee island where her own da had helped build a lighthouse. The light went out, and the fog moved in, just as it has this time. Just as it did before, as young Albert here has told you, I'm sure."

A cloud passed in front of the sun again, shrouding the room in shadows, and Bel, who was used to the fog, to the sea, to the changing skies, fought the urge to scoot even closer to Nolie.

"It was much as it is now," Maggie continued. "At first, no one paid it too much mind. There had been fog on the sea before. And then it moved closer. Then it *took*. Boats, villagers, eventually a fishing hut on the shore. When whispers of witchcraft began to spread, my father sent his men to light the lighthouse; they never came back. Then the braver lads of the village went."

At Bel's left, Al sat up a little straighter, and Bel remembered that in Al's own time, his brother had been a brave lad who tried to light the lamp.

"And then one day, I was walking along the shore, looking out at the fog, and I came across a wee boat. Called the *Selkie*."

Maggie took another sip of her tea, and Nolie and Bel exchanged a look just as Al leaned closer, resting his elbows on his knees. "That was the boat they'd sent Cait off in," Maggie continued. "And I . . . I knew that the *Selkie* had come back for me. That I was the only one who could put this all to rights." Maggie's knobby fingers tightened around her mug, her gaze seeming far away all of a sudden. "Cait had been my friend. If she had been a witch, if she *had* cursed us all, I thought perhaps she'd talk to me.

That she'd *sent* for me. And so I went. I made my way to the island, climbed the stone steps of the lighthouse, and lit the lamp."

"Did you see Cait?" Nolie asked, leaning forward.

Maggie shook her head. "I can't remember. I know that sounds mad, but—"

"The fog does something to you," Al added. He wasn't looking at any of them, his eyes still focused somewhere around his feet.

"Indeed," Maggie said. "Makes things harder to remember. Anyway, no, I can't recall seeing Cait, but I know I lit that lamp. And when I tried to row out . . ."

She trailed off, swallowing hard before taking a sip of tea. Her voice sounded rougher when she continued, "As your friend Albert said, the fog does things to your mind. Time stops having meaning. You row and never go anywhere. Until one day, the fog simply . . . let me go. As it did you, Albert."

Bel glanced over at Al, who was staring at Maggie, mouth gone slack.

"It was you," he said, and Bel saw his hands clench on his knees. "When the fog came to Journey's End in . . . in my time, there was a meeting, kept all secret-like. And there was a girl there I didn't know. You."

Maggie rested her free hand on the arm of her chair. "Aye, 'twas me. The people of Journey's End didn't know what to do with me, of course, so they kept it all as secret as they could. Gave me this house, as it was on what had been by father's land. Set me up with a small trust so that I might live the rest of my days in some comfort. The priest came every day to help with schooling, to teach me English. I only spoke Gaelic when I returned, of course. And eventually, Journey's End forgot who I was or how long I'd been here. They only knew I'd *always* been here."

"And all this sweet stuff?" Nolie asked, gesturing around to the TV, the laptop, the tablet. "Is there, like, a special fund for you to get to buy all the electronics?"

Maggie shook her head, laughing. "Ah, no, this is my own doing. That trust grew into a quite a tidy sum over time, and I like all these things. Even after all these years, they still feel a bit like magic, I suppose."

Bel could see where that made sense, and suddenly she had a thousand questions she wanted to ask. How far away did Maggie's sixteenth-century childhood seem, and what had Journey's End been like then? Did she walk past the ruins of her father's castle every day and remember walking the halls?

But there would have to be time for that later. Maggie was already settling back into her chair. "'Twas I who had the plaque made in the city center for Cait once I'd been back a decade or so. I knew it couldn't make up for what had happened to her, but . . . I had to try."

"*In Hope of Forgiveness*," Bel murmured. "That was you. For Cait."

Maggie was turning her mug this way and that in her hands, and she didn't look over at Bel. "Aye, it was. It seemed like such a small thing, given all that happened to her, but it were the best I could do at the time."

She sat there for a moment, lost in her own thoughts, before shaking her head. "Anyway, that seems to be the way of it. The light is lit, the fog pulls back, and the person who lit the lamp remains trapped in the fog. Until the light goes out again, of course. And now here we are, Albert MacLeish. The people who saved our village, watching it happen all over again."

"Okay." Nolie leaned forward, setting her tea on the table with a thump. "So you went to light the lamp in 1553 when you were how old?"

"Ten and three," Maggie answered, and Nolie tugged on one ear.

"That's a weird way to say thirteen, but fine. And then you got kicked out or freed or whatever in 1918. Even if being in the fog keeps you young while you're in it, you would've been thirteen in 1918. Which means you should be, like, *super* old. No offense."

Maggie chuckled at that, inclining her head at Nolie. "None taken. And you're right. I only began to age again once I'd come out of the fog, but I aged . . . slowly, I suppose you'd say. I can only suppose it has something to do with the fog itself."

She said it lightly, like it was no big deal that the fog had altered the way her entire *body* worked, but Al clearly wasn't taking that casually.

"So it'll be the same for me?" he asked. "I'll not grow up like normal?"

Maggie narrowed her blue eyes, studying him. "Can't rightly say," she finally answered. "I was in the fog for near on five hundred years. You were in less than a hundred. Perhaps you'll only end up a few months behind."

Nolie leaned over Bel. "Albert, I promise we'll still be your friends even if you're permanently in seventh grade. Or at least until we're grown-ups."

Maggie gave another one of those rusty laughs even as Albert scowled at Nolie, folding his arms over his chest.

Bel patted their knees, saying, "Okay, now is not the time for this." She looked back at Maggie. "So the *Selkie* came to you, and that's what let you light the light. All those other people. They just headed out in other boats, and never lit the lamp *or* came back."

"Like my brother," Al said quietly. He was looking down at the carpet again, his hair falling over his brow. Then he lifted his gaze, looking at Nolie and Bel, then at Maggie. "But then I found the *Selkie*, too. And I . . . I felt like I had to go."

Maggie got up from her chair, her bones creaking slightly as she busied herself cleaning up their tea things. "So that's it, then," she said. "The trick of it. I always wondered."

"They sent Cait off in the *Selkie*," Nolie said slowly. "But it came back, and got *you*. You lit the lamp, but then when it went out again, *you* came back, and *Albert* found the *Selkie*."

"And now the light is out a third time, and Albert has returned," Maggie supplied, straightening up and taking in the three of them on the sofa.

"So the question now is simple," Maggie said. "Who has the *Selkie* come for?"

CHAPTER 26

BEL LED THE WAY BACK DOWN TO THE BEACH, SHOVING her hands in her pockets to keep them warm, hoping that if she kept moving fast enough, she wouldn't have time to get scared. What she was about to do was definitely something worth being scared about, after all, but Nolie and Al were following her, neither saying anything, and she hoped that meant they had the same idea about what had to happen next.

Bel didn't even pause until they got to the beach, right near the little cave where Al had been hiding and where the *Selkie* was still beached.

Turning, Bel faced her friends and put her hands on her hips.

"So it's us," she said. "Who have to light the light. The *Selkie* came to both of us." Bel said it as fast as she could, but also tried to make it sound as firm as the rocks around them. That was a trick she'd learned from what her mum always said: Say things like you don't expect an argument, and you won't get one. Bel reckoned a woman with four kids, three of them boys, had learned that lesson well.

"The *Selkie* is such a *little* boat," Nolie said, and Bel almost wanted to laugh. Of *course* it was the boat that scared Nolie, not the fog.

"You heard Maggie," Bel said, tugging the sleeves of her jumper over her fingers. "It's the only thing to do, and the only way we can save Dad and Jaime. And your dad, too."

"Except we might not come back."

"There is that part," she said, "but think about it. No one has ever gone as a *group* before. Maybe that makes it different."

She saw Nolie and Al exchange a look, and quickly added, "Not a group, a *pair*." The *Selkie* had already come for Al once. Who knew what might happen if he went again? It seemed like too much to risk. "Al, you'll have to stay here."

"Not too likely," Al fired back, drawing himself up to his full height. Over the past few weeks, his hair had gotten longer, shaggier, and now it hung over his brow until he pushed it back with an impatient hand. "If we do this, we should all go," he said.

This time, it was Nolie who objected. "Except that the fog ate you before."

"But I was able to light the light," he said. Their words were loud and echoing in the cave, but Bel could still hear the pound of the surf outside. "Neither of you have ever done that before. When I went out, I already knew how."

Nolie reached out with one toe, nudging some loose pebbles. "Right, but it's not like it's some brand-new lighthouse with technology. It's just . . . lighting something the old-fashioned way, right?"

Al snorted, thrusting his hands into his pockets. "If ye think that's all there is to it, all the more reason for me to come as well."

He had a point, but Bel couldn't let them descend into an argument. "Nolie, you don't have to go. Maybe Al is right, and—"

"No." Nolie shook her head fiercely, and Bel could see that once again her braid was coming unraveled. "I was there when we found the *Selkie*, too. It came to me just as much as it did to you. We're a team."

And when she said that, something in Bel's chest seemed to bloom open like a flower. She's never been on someone's team before. There were so few kids in Journey's End, and hardly any girls. From the moment Nolie had walked into the store, Bel had known they'd be friends, and sitting in that cave with her and Al, she suddenly felt like it was right that she and Nolie finish this together. Hadn't it all started when Nolie showed up? That couldn't just be a coincidence.

"What are you going to do?" Al asked, sitting down on one of the nearby rocks. "Do ye even have something to light it with?"

Bel's fingers curled around the box of matches Maggie had given her before they'd left her house. She had waited until Nolie and Al were already out the door, and she hadn't said a word, simply pressing the box into Bel's hands. It was the closest thing to a seal of approval Bel was going to get.

"Okay," she said. "All three of us. It makes sense. Al lit the lamp before, this is my village, and . . . well, we must need you, too, Nol."

Nolie crossed her arms, the vinyl of her slicker squeaking. "Could be I'm just the friend who tragically bites it in the course of saving the day. I know y'all don't get a lot of movies and TV out here, but there's always one person on these kinds of quests that gets totally killed. And it *would* be me, because I'm the funny one. It's always the funny one."

"I don't think I want to watch your movies and TV if funny people are getting killed," Al commented, giving Nolie a smile. "I like the funny ones."

Her cheeks turning pink, Nolie shrugged and looked away, and Bel hid her own smile as she looked down at the journal spread open in front of her. "No one is going to get killed on this trip, funny or not," she said very firmly.

"All of this happened for a reason. Al coming back, Nolie coming to Journey's End, me . . . well, me always being here, I s'pose. We're here to finally put this right."

"Even though putting it right means putting our parents out of jobs," Nolie said, and Bel frowned. She didn't like to think of that part of it, but it couldn't be helped now.

Then Nolie heaved a sigh, rubbing her hands together. "Okay, so just so y'all know, if I get killed on this, I'm going to haunt you both. Even Albert, who is technically part ghost himself anyway."

Al frowned. "Ain not."

"Albert, please come to terms with your ghostiness," Nolie said, making an exaggerated sad face as she patted him on the arm, and Bel rolled her eyes at both of them.

"All three of us are going to be ghosts if we don't get going," Bel reminded them. "You heard Maggie, once the fog starts moving in closer, there's not much time left."

The three of them turned then, looking back out at the water and at the Boundary. Somewhere inside all that roiling gray was her father's boat, and a rocky island with an old lighthouse. A light she had to light.

And she had no idea how she was going to do it.

CHAPTER 27

BEL RECKONED THE *SELKIE* MIGHT HAVE BEEN A NICE boat in 1553, and it certainly held up well considering how old it was, but that didn't mean she felt any better about getting in it and shoving off into the actual ocean.

Clutching the side of the boat, she reminded herself that she was a girl born on the sea, who came from a long line of sailors. She'd been on her father's boat for years, and she wasn't going to let this scare her.

Still, it was one thing to tell herself that, another to feel like the little boat beneath her wanted to get away. Wanted to plunge back into the fog it came from.

"I really hate this," Nolie said softly as Albert clambered into the boat. "Just so you know."

Bel looked at Nolie, swaddled in her slicker, and made herself smile.

"Bet this isn't what you planned for your summer vacation."

For the first time since they'd left Maggie's, Nolie smiled, looking more like herself.

"Oh, no, this is exactly how I thought it would go. You know, see my dad in Scotland, hear some bagpipes, sail off to fight a ghost witch, light a magic lighthouse, and save our dads."

That made Bel smile, too, and better than that, it made her feel brave.

Still, she held tight to Nolie's hand, and Albert rowed the boat farther offshore.

It was a gray day today, like most days in Journey's End, and Bel found herself wondering if she'd remember what happened today. Looking around now, forgetting seemed impossible. How could she forget the smooth gray of the sky, the deep slate of the sea?

The boat was carried aloft on a swell then, and Bel felt Nolie's hand clutch hers tighter. She swallowed hard, looking ahead of her.

But ahead was the fog, and while Bel had been closer to it than this before—she'd been out on her dad's boat more times than she could count—this felt different.

Albert looked over his shoulder at the Boundary, and when he turned back to them, his thin arms working hard to row them faster, he said, "This is like I remember."

Bel was about to ask what he meant by that, but then

she could feel it, too. The day had already been windy and cold, but now it felt even chillier, and more than that, there was a feeling to the air, a sort of charge that had the hairs on the back of her neck standing up.

"Bel," Nolie murmured.

"What, Nolie?"

"Remind me that jumping overboard right now is a bad idea."

The fog rose up above them, thick and dense and roiling. They were close to it now, almost as close as Bel had ever been.

"It's a bad idea," she said to Nolie. "Because you'd drown."

"Not sure that would be worse than this," Nolie muttered.

There was a soft clacking sound as Albert drew up the oars, and Bel frowned at him. This close to the Boundary, her skin seemed to itch, and she felt that same feeling she'd had earlier by the shore, that need to go as fast as she could before she lost her nerve.

"Why aren't you rowing?" she asked, and Albert shook his head.

"Like I said, this is how it was last time," he told her, voice so soft she could barely hear him over the waves and the wind and the rush of blood in her ears.

"This, I remember. You can't row into it," he continued, his arms folded. "It has to draw you in."

Nolie dropped Bel's hand.

For long, long moments, they sat there on the boat, feeling it rock in the waves, listening to the splash of water against the hull. It was one of the worst feelings Bel had ever felt, that wait. Just like before, it gave her time to think, and she knew that was the worst thing you could have when doing something like this. Time to think meant time to reconsider, and they didn't have that right now.

The *Selkie* had come to them, and whether they wanted that responsibility or not, it was theirs now.

But then she felt the boat slide forward.

It wasn't a lurch, nothing like the violent bucking she'd felt when they first rowed out. This was more like there was an invisible rope tied to the boat.

Nolie felt it, too, Bel could tell. Her hands curled around Bel's again, fingers cold, grip tight. At the front of the boat, Albert sat very still except for his fingers, still drumming on his legs.

The boat slid over the water, and with one smooth tug, they were pulled forward, the fog enveloping them.

CHAPTER 28

AS SOON AS THE FOG CLOSED OVER THEM, EVERYTHING went silent. It was the strangest thing Nolie had ever felt, and her ears were suddenly full, like someone had stuffed them with cotton.

Bel was right in front of her, but she could hardly see her; only the bright red of her own hair was visible in the mist. Albert was little more than a shape, and Nolie tugged at the straps of her backpack.

Like that was going to help her now.

The boat was still being pulled forward, she thought, but it was hard to tell since the fog kept moving around them, pressing damply against her skin, and Nolie realized she was taking quick, shallow breaths.

"I don't want to breathe it in," she told Bel, who nodded, still looking around her.

"It's like being in a cloud," Bel said, but Nolie didn't agree. Sure, it reminded her of being on planes, caught in high clouds, but there was something different about this fog. She'd felt it from the day she'd gotten to Journey's End, and she definitely felt it now.

"My dad says magic and science are the same thing sometimes," she said to Bel, "but I think he's wrong. There's nothing 'science' about this."

She wondered where her dad was now. Wondered whether, after they got him back—and they would get him back—he'd pack up and leave the Institute, knowing there was no way he would ever be able to figure out what this was.

This, Nolie knew, was magic, pure and simple.

They kept floating, the boat rocking gently, the fog never thinning, or getting any thicker, either, just there, a real thing almost solid, and Nolie peered through it, hoping to see something. But there was nothing except fog and fog and more fog, rolling out in front of them.

"What would happen if we rowed out now?" she asked, surprised to find she was whispering.

But Bel whispered back. "I don't think we *can* row back," she replied. "Which way would we even go?"

It was a good question. Everything looked exactly the same in all directions.

"That's the thing," Albert said from the front of the boat, and Nolie heard the creak of the oars as he rested his elbows on them. "This deep in, there is no out. No in, either, I s'pose."

"Do you remember getting this far last time?" Nolie asked, and she could make out Albert nodding.

"Aye. But not much past it, to tell the truth."

"Super ace rad," Nolie muttered as the boat continued to rock in the eerily still water. It didn't even feel like the ocean anymore. She had spent enough time watching the Caillte Sea to know that it was rough with waves most of the time. This water was more like a lake, and something about it felt so *wrong* that Nolie swallowed hard, wanting to wrap her arms tight around herself.

But the boat kept moving, and even though she was more terrified than she'd ever been in her entire life, Nolie couldn't help but look at all that fog and think, *We did it.* Even just talking about it had seemed crazy, like something out of a scary story. Definitely not a thing people *did.* But they had. Her, Bel and Al. And suddenly, no matter how scared she was or how badly this might go—and Nolie was worried it was going to go really, really badly—she and Bel had been brave enough to try. Just like Albert had all those years ago.

"I'm serious," Nolie said, not quite so afraid now. "This is going to make the best 'how I spent my summer vacation' essay *ever.* Do y'all have those in—"

The boat suddenly juddered, the bottom scraping hard against something, and Nolie let out a panicked shriek, grabbing the sides of the boat with both hands, the rough wood cutting into her palms.

Al said something that sounded like a string of hissing and choking, so Nolie guessed it was Gaelic, and probably pretty bad words in Gaelic at that, if his tone of voice was anything to go by. Only Bel was quiet, twisting around to look over her shoulder.

Once she stopped feeling like she might throw up, Nolie also raised her head, following the direction of Bel's gaze.

For the first time, Nolie could see something more than fog—she could see rocky green hills rising up from the water, high enough that she had to crane her neck to look up at the top of them.

And there at the top, rising out of the fog and mist, was a lighthouse.

"It's real," Bel said, her voice loud in her ears.

It was a silly thing to say, all told, seeing as how the lighthouse was sitting right in front of them—well, in front and slightly above—but a part of Bel had believed there was simply no way this island and that lighthouse could be real.

But now they *had* to light the light.

And if the lighthouse was real, that meant that Cait was probably real, too. That somewhere up this rocky beach, there was an actual witch waiting for them.

Bel bit her bottom lip. *One thing at a time.*

Al was already climbing out of the boat, nearly stumbling because he was in such a hurry, and Bel followed a little more slowly, the cold water sloshing over her shoes. Behind her, she heard Nolie getting out, too, and she helped her friend tug the boat farther up onto shore. It was clear that Al wasn't going to be any help with that. He was still staring up at the lighthouse. There was no sun here, no sky. Just the endless gray of the Boundary, wrapping around the island like a bubble, and Bel's heart pounded hard in her chest.

"It's so quiet," Al said, and Bel looked over at him. The air was still here, too, so there was no wind, no sound of surf crashing. "'Twas quiet the last time, but I'd forgotten."

"'Twas cursed by witch fog," Nolie said, coming to stand between Bel and Al. "'Twas," she repeated. "I'm going to use that word a lot more. Provided we don't die here, obviously."

"Obviously," Bel and Al echoed at the same time.

Then they stood there a bit longer, still looking up at the lighthouse.

Not surprisingly, it was Nolie who broke the silence. "So do we go up there first?" she asked. "Or look for the boats?"

Al startled, like Nolie was waking him from a dream, and then he cleared his throat. "Up to the pair of ye."

Bel looked over at Nolie, and tucked her blond hair behind her ear. "Maybe we can't find them without the light first," she said. "So we should do that, I s'pose."

Nolie glanced up at the lighthouse. "Probably."

Al dusted his hands on his pants. "Aye," he said, and Nolie repeated that word, too.

"Before I leave here, I'm going to be saying all the Scottish words," she told them, the three of them making their way up the rocky path from the beach toward the lighthouse.

Bel was thankful for Nolie's chatter, since it kept her from being scared. Well, kept her from being *too* scared. As they got closer and closer to the lighthouse, Bel's mouth felt drier and drier, her knees shakier. The path wound around a bit, dipping between hills or boulders near the size of houses, but the lighthouse was always there, dark and unseeing.

And then suddenly they were there, standing in front of the door. It was made of old, weathered wood, the handle a ring of rusting iron.

Nolie stepped a little closer to Bel, her boots crunching on the path of loose pebbles. "Three of us," she said. "Three is a lucky number."

Then she turned to Bel, raising her eyebrows. "I read that somewhere. Do you think it's true?"

Reaching out one trembling hand, Bel pushed the door, hearing it creak and feeling it give.

"S'pose we're about to find out."

CHAPTER 29

STANDING JUST INSIDE THE LIGHTHOUSE, NOLIE LOOKED around. The air smelled heavy somehow, like a place that had been closed up for a long time, and her skin felt clammy and damp. Similar to the castle ruins near Maggie's, the stones seemed to be holding in the cold, letting it seep out until she had goose bumps even though she was wearing a jacket.

There wasn't much to the lighthouse, really. It seemed to be just a tall, round tower. Stairs curled up one side, carved of the same dark stone as the rest of the lighthouse, and there were grooves in each step, like hundreds of years of footsteps had worn away the rock.

Except no one had been in here in hundreds of years besides Albert and Maggie, and they'd only lit the light and left. Had it been the girl? The ghost? Pacing this dim, cold place?

The thought made Nolie want to run, to get out.

Behind her, Albert stepped closer. "What now?" she asked him. Bel was still standing just inside the door, looking out into the fog behind them.

Albert looked up at the top of the tower. There were big, arched windows carved out there, letting in the gray light, and Nolie could see a sort of small platform where the steps ended. In what light there was in the tower, it looked charred and blackened.

"We go up there," Albert replied, nodding at that platform. "There's a lantern. We light it, and then—"

"And then we maybe get stuck in the fog forever trying to row out," Nolie finished.

"It let us in," Bel reminded her, coming into the chamber. She left the door open, and the fog curled in after her, twining around her ankles like a cat.

"We got this far, which has to mean something."

Nolie nodded. She was doing this for her dad, to save him, but what if she never got out, either? What would her mom do without her?

"I'm surprised you didn't bring a camera," Bel said to her, coming up close enough to nudge Nolie with her elbow. "Bet your *Spirit Chasers* show has never been anywhere as ace as this."

Nolie smiled despite her shivers. "I don't know, they did an episode in an asylum that was pretty freaky, but this would have to come in a close second. Could shoot up to first place if we actually see a ghost."

Albert was already walking toward the steps, but he paused, looking over his shoulder at both of them. "I never saw anything when I was here the last time, far as I remember. But maybe she'll make a special appearance for you, Nolie."

"Yay," Nolie replied, wishing she felt something more than scared. A camera would've been nice, actually, but not so she could record whatever happened. So she could have something to hide behind. Looking at all of this through a lens would've made it feel like a TV show, not the scariest thing she'd ever done.

But as Albert began moving up the stairs, she made herself follow behind him, Bel taking up the rear.

"All for one, one for all," Nolie said. "That's from a book."

Albert gave her what she was now beginning to think of as his signature scowl, his dark brows lowering over his eyes, corners of his mouth turning down so sharply it was almost funny.

"I know that," he said. "That book is older than me."

Shrugging, Nolie shoved her hands in her pockets. "Just keeping you on your toes."

"Can all of your toes hurry up?" Bel said from behind

Nolie. "The sooner this is over, the sooner we can get home."

"Do you remember this bit?" Nolie asked as they wound their way up. "I mean, the fog felt all familiar. So, does this?" The stairs were so narrow her shoulder brushed the wall, and while heights had never really bugged her, she kept her eyes firmly on Albert's shoulders, not the ever-increasing drop on her other side.

"Summat?" Albert replied, and Nolie guessed that was old-timey for "kinda."

"It's like . . . you know when you wake up from a dream, and for the first bit you're awake, everything you dreamed is clear? But then you lie there, and it all starts to fade? That's what my memory of this place is like."

"It feels like a dream for me, too," Bel said, and Nolie dared a glance behind her. Bel had paused a few steps back and was looking down toward the open door. More fog had slid in now, creeping along the floor, and Nolie had the uneasy feeling it was slithering after them.

"Okay, let's get a move on," she said, fighting the urge to start shoving Albert up the stairs.

They moved up and up until finally, just in front of one of the arches cut from the stone, the stairs stopped at the little platform.

And there, in the center, was the light.

Or what Nolie assumed was the light.

"This is it?" Nolie looked at the glass cylinder on the platform. It covered a pile of sticks and rags, and it didn't seem like a light strong enough to push away magical fog, but then, it was clearly magic, too, so what did she know?

Taking the box of matches from Bel, Albert studied the lamp, but didn't lift the glass.

"What is it?" Bel asked. She was still standing behind Nolie, closest to the edge of the platform.

Albert shook his head, his hair falling over his forehead. "Just . . . I got this far last time. I lit it. I remember that. And after . . ."

He didn't have to say what had happened after. They all knew.

"Do it," Nolie said, looking out the window. There was nothing to see, nothing but gray. No water, no sky. Just this endless fog, and in that second, she didn't care if they never got away from the island. If the light would get rid of the fog, that's all that mattered. Anything but this never-ending mist.

Nodding, Albert reached out and lifted the glass.

Suddenly, a wind blew in through the window. It was less like a breeze and more like a solid thing hitting them, smelling like the ocean and old stone, and it was hard enough to make Nolie's eyes water.

"What—" she started as she lifted a hand against it, but before she could say anything else, there was a cry from behind her.

The wind was still blowing as Nolie turned to see Bel fall off the ledge and down toward the stone floor below.

CHAPTER 30

BEL CLUTCHED AT THE ROCK, HER NAILS DIGGING IN. She'd just managed to catch hold of one of the stairs a few steps below the platform. Her palms stung, and her shoulder muscles ached, but that was nothing compared to the panic spiraling in her stomach as her feet kicked over empty air.

"I've got you!" she heard Nolie say, and she could feel her friend's fingers curling around her wrists, holding her in place. Nolie's hands were nearly as cold as the rock beneath Bel's fingers, and she squeezed her eyes shut, trying to breathe more slowly, to not let panic make her claw at the rock and swing her legs harder.

Another hand closed over her elbow, and Bel opened her eyes to see Al on his knees next to Nolie, his face pale.

Both Al and Nolie held on to Bel, but without anywhere to put her feet, she couldn't seem to get enough leverage to shove herself back up on the stair.

"We'll pull you up," Nolie said, but when she tugged at Bel, Bel's palm slid against the damp rock, making her nearly lose her grip.

"Stop!" she cried, and so much for not panicking, because her voice sounded thin and high.

But Nolie was still holding her, and Al's grip tightened on Bel's elbow, so even as her legs dangled over the space, she could feel them working together to pull her back up.

Then Nolie gasped, her grip on Bel suddenly slipping.

"Nolie!"

"Sorry, sorry," Nolie replied, her hands tightening again on Bel's wrists. "I got distracted."

Even though she was pretty sure she was seconds away from throwing up, Bel managed to say, "What's more distracting than me almost falling to my death?"

"There's a ghost behind you," Nolie answered, and Bel gritted her teeth, holding on.

"I know," she said. "That's why I fell."

"It pushed you?" Al asked, breathing hard as he kept pulling at Bel, but Bel shook her head.

"No. No, I saw it, and I just . . ."

She had stepped back without thinking as the form rushed through the window, her brain refusing to process what it was seeing, and that's why she had fallen. But that sounded silly out loud, so Bel just hung on.

By the time they'd pulled Bel back onto the ledge, she was breathing hard, her heart was still racing, and there was blood on her palms.

Still, all of that was nothing compared to how she felt when she could finally turn around, still on her hands and knees, and really see the figure currently floating just beyond the stairs.

It was a girl, and one not much older than Bel or Nolie. Her hair was long and red, floating around her face, and her brown dress looked old and worn. The fog hovered all around her, curling beneath her feet, draping over her shoulders.

"I've waited my whole life to see a ghost," Nolie breathed, and Bel looked over at her. Nolie was sitting, her back against the wall, her eyes wide; beside her, Al had risen to his feet, also staring at the girl.

"Did you see her before?" Bel asked him, wondering if it was rude to talk about the ghost like she wasn't there. But she hardly seemed to hear them, simply staring at the three of them, her hands out to her sides, her expression blank.

"Not that I recall," Al answered, and Nolie rose to her feet, too.

"I bet you'd recall a ghost," she said. "And if you didn't, we can't be friends anymore."

"Go," Bel said, standing up. "Light the light. Hurry. *Now.*"

The ghost—*Cait*, Bel remembered—didn't say anything, but her head swung toward Bel, eyes watching.

"Hurry!" Bel cried again, and Al started scrambling up the steps again. Bel went to follow him, but Nolie grabbed her arm.

"Wait," she said, and when Bel stood there, staring at her, she added, "Aren't you going to talk to her?"

Bel looked again at the figure still hovering above the ground, real and unreal all at once, and all the bravery she'd summoned up to get out here seemed to desert her. "We're here to light the light," she reminded Nolie. "We have to do that."

"We're also here to help our dads," Nolie said. "And hopefully not get stuck here. We can't do that if we don't *talk* to her."

And then Nolie flashed her crooked grin, shaking her head. "Oh man, now I get it. I know exactly why y'all need me."

With that, she twisted to get her backpack and pulled it off her shoulders. "Go on," she called up to Al. "Light it. I have an idea."

"Ghosts hang around because they have unfinished business," she told Bel. "And Cait here probably has tons of it, what with being unjustly murdered. That's, like, the *number one reason* people haunt places. We just have to show her . . ."

Nolie trailed off, and Bel looked back up at Al, who was fumbling with the matches.

"Go help him," Nolie told her, then looked back to Cait. For all that Nolie had looked pale and terrified on the boat, she now seemed as brave as Bel had ever seen anyone be, her shoulders back, her gaze steady. Only her hands, shaking slightly as they clutched *Legends of the North*, gave her away.

Bel gave Nolie one last squeeze on her shoulder, then hurried up the stairs to Al.

Taking a deep breath, Nolie faced her first ghost.

"Hi," she said weakly, then cleared her throat, making her voice stronger. "Hello, I mean. I'm Nolie Stanhope, and I'm . . . not from around here. But my dad lives in Journey's End, and now he's somewhere on this island. Or at least I think he is, and I'm really hoping you can help us out with that."

There was no reaction from Cait, and Nolie got the impression that most of her focus was on Bel and Albert, still struggling to light the lamp. Two matches had already gone out, far as Nolie could tell, and Albert was saying more bad words in Gaelic as he fished another one out of the box.

"We know what happened to you," Nolie went on, and now she had Cait's attention, even if she wasn't sure Cait could understand what she was saying. "How they put you out in a boat to die for something you didn't do. And you *totally* got a raw deal. Not . . . that you know what that means. But look. Other people know it now, too."

Leaning forward, she offered a look at the book to Cait. The ghost didn't move, but Nolie didn't let that discourage her. "It's here," she said, pointing to the page titled "The Sad Tale of Cait McInnish." "You see?" Nolie asked, tapping the pages. "The real story is out there. People know. And the people in the village . . . they're sorry. Look." She flipped the page to the black-and-white illustration of the little plaque near the harbor. "This says, *In Hope of Forgiveness*. Maggie McLeod put it there. Maggie was your friend, right?"

Cait's ghost continued staring at her, and Nolie's nerve nearly deserted her. Squaring her shoulders, she made herself go on. "I know it's not the whole town, and I know it doesn't have your name on it or anything, but we could fix that. And I'm not saying you have to stop with the fog—it would be better if you didn't, really," she added, thinking of her dad and Bel's. "But just this one time, if you could let us light the light and find our families and let us go, I'd . . . *we'd* all really appreciate it."

As far as stirring speeches went, it wasn't much, and

Nolie didn't think the guys on *Spirit Chasers* would be very proud of her, but it was all she had. Bel and Al may have been braver about coming out here in the boat, but if there was one thing Nolie knew, it was ghosts.

"Please," she added.

For a long moment, Cait hovered there, and then Nolie heard a shout from above her.

She turned, and as she watched, Al lowered a lit match to the bundle of sticks and rags there at the top of the tower. Bel held the glass cylinder in her hands, and at last, a little fire kindled to life.

The lamp was lit.

Relief flooded through Nolie, making her limbs weak, her hands shaking so much she almost dropped the book. "Oh, y'all are *awesome*," she called up to them both, and Albert rewarded her with a grin. Bel put the glass back over the flame, and then they both walked back to where Nolie stood, still facing Cait.

"One thing down," Bel said.

"Hardest bit to go," Albert added, his gaze wary as he watched the ghost.

Cait was still floating there, staring at the book. Nolie had no idea if she could read it, or if she even understood what Nolie had said to her.

But then she lifted her eyes, taking in all three of them, and something passed over her face. In that moment, she didn't look scary or even ghostly. She looked like a girl, and a sad one at that.

And then she pointed a long arm out to the right.

Nolie blinked, closing the book. "What is that? Is that where they are? That . . . general direction?"

She looked back up the stairs at Bel and Albert, both of whom were looking the direction Cait was pointing.

"Is that it?" Nolie asked again.

But Cait had already vanished, leaving the tower quiet and cold.

CHAPTER 31

PEBBLES RATTLED UNDERFOOT AS NOLIE RAN FROM THE lighthouse, Bel and Albert close behind. Already there were patches appearing in the fog overhead, bits of blue sky revealing themselves. Her heart was still racing, and her eyes darted around, looking for any sign of the boats. Cait had told them where to find their families, she was sure of it, but she wasn't as sure that meant they were being freed. So she wanted to get her dad and get out of here as quickly as she could.

Nolie was moving so quickly that she didn't notice the object sticking out of the sand until she was running straight at it, then tripping, her arms pinwheeling as she fell.

"Oof!" she breathed, hitting the beach. Bel and Albert ran over to help her.

"I'm fine," Nolie said immediately, going to stand up, but then she looked down to see what she'd tripped over. "Is that—"

Bel pulled the object up out of the rocks and sand. It was rusty and the gold on the hilt was barely shining, but there was no doubt that it was a sword, probably a really nice one at one point.

"The heck?" Nolie asked, and Albert straightened up, looking around.

"From the men Maggie's father sent," he said. "There must be all sorts of things left about."

There wasn't much time to see if that was true, as far as Nolie was concerned. They needed to find the boats and get out of there, but Albert was moving over the beach, his eyes searching.

"Al!" Bel called. "We have to go!"

"I know!" he replied, but he was still walking in the opposite direction from them, hands in his pockets, head down, scanning the rocks and sand.

"What is he—" Nolie started, rising to her feet, but Bel stopped her with a hand on her arm.

"His brother," she reminded Nolie. "He's seeing if there's anything of his."

Everything in Nolie was itching to get to the other side of the island, but Albert had come with them, back to this place that had taken so much from him.

They owed him a few minutes.

And sure enough, after just a little bit of waiting, Al squatted down and plucked something dark from the pebbles. It was a navy-blue cap, and Nolie and Bel stood there, watching him brush it off before he sat it on his head. When he came back to them, his eyes were bright, and Nolie felt her own throat constrict. She might've hugged him in that moment, but he sniffed hard and nodded in the direction of the other side of the island. "Come on," he said. "We have some rescuing to do."

The island was tiny, so walking around to the side where Cait had pointed didn't take them long, but it still felt like a lifetime to Nolie. What if the boats weren't there? What if what Cait had meant was *Oh, yeah, I sunk those boats like the rest, just over that way*?

But then they rounded a tall, rocky outcrop and there, resting on the beach, waves lapping over the hull, were the two boats: the *Bonny Bel*, and the smaller, slighter *Caillte Cruise*.

Nolie ran, feet skidding on the rocks, and from the corner of her eye, she saw Bel sprinting for her family's boat.

There was a metal ladder affixed to the side of the *Caillte Cruise*, and Nolie splashed out into the shallow water to get to it, her legs feeling numb from the cold almost immediately. But she barely noticed the cold as she heaved her way up the ladder and onto the boat.

She saw Dave first, the bright red of his cap easy to spot where he lay on the deck. Then her eyes landed on her dad, curled on his side just past Dave, almost like he was taking a nap.

A sob burst out of Nolie's throat as she ran forward and fell onto her knees there on the deck, her hand going to her dad's shoulder.

"Dad!" she cried, shaking him hard. For too long—five heartbeats, a bunch of harsh breaths—her dad was still and silent. And then, finally, she felt him stir.

"Nolie?" her dad asked, his voice raspy. He was blinking at her, looking like he was coming out of a dream.

Nolie felt tears run down her cheeks, and she nodded quickly, needing to hold it together.

"It's okay, Dad," she said. "It's okay, we found you. And now we need to wake up Dave and get the heck out of here."

Her dad sat up slowly, a hand to the back of his head, and then he looked around, confused. "Where are we?" he asked, but Nolie had already moved over to Dave, who was groaning as she shook him awake.

"The little island," she said, "with the lighthouse. But Dad, it's going to be dark soon, so—"

"The island?" her dad repeated, and now he definitely looked awake, blue eyes bright behind his glasses. "Wait, Nol, we can't leave yet. I'd like to see that lighthouse for myself."

Dave was finally awake, blinking and confused like her

dad had been, so Nolie turned her attention back to her dad, who was already on his feet.

"We need to go," she said, standing up, too. "I know, I know, science and observation, all very awesome, but, Dad, can we just ... please, I want to go home now."

Her dad stopped at that, looking at her, and Nolie held her breath.

Then he gave a quick nod, coming over to help Dave to his feet. "Of course, honey," he told Nolie. "Of course we can go home."

Breathing a sigh of relief, Nolie left her dad and Dave for a second, rushing to the rail of the boat. Several feet away, Bel, her dad, and her brother were all on their feet on the deck of the *Bonny Bel*, and Nolie waved to them. Bel waved back, then cupped her hands around her mouth and shouted, "Ready?"

Glancing back over her shoulder, Nolie saw Dave making his way to the front of the boat, and she gave Bel a thumbs-up before shouting out, "Where's Albert?"

But even as she asked it, she saw him, still standing on the beach, his brother's hat in his hands.

Boys, Nolie thought, then she turned to her dad, saying, "I'll be right back."

"Nolie!" her dad called, but she was already scrambling back down the ladder and through the freezing water, moving as fast as she could.

"Climb aboard, matey, or aye-aye, or whatever we're supposed to say at times like this," Nolie said as she reached him, and Albert smiled at her, but he was still twisting his brother's cap around in his hands.

"You're not . . . you're not thinking you're going to *stay* here, are you?" Nolie asked, every bit of her suddenly cold, and not from the water.

Albert's shoulders rolled underneath his shirt. "I'm scared, Nolie," he said. The words were plain, his tone flat, but as Nolie looked into his dark eyes, she could see just how much he meant them.

"The last time I left this island, I came back to a world where everything I knew was different. Where everyone I loved was . . ."

Albert's throat moved, and when he started talking about it, his voice sounded huskier. "I like the new world I ended up in, I truly do, and I want to go back. But what if we can't? What if I lose that, too?"

Without thinking, Nolie reached out and grabbed his free hand, the one not holding his brother's cap. "You're not alone this time," she said, squeezing his fingers. "You're coming with us. And when we get back to Journey's End, we're going to teach you more about the internet and video games and TV and books, and anything else you want to learn. But we have to go now, Al. Please."

His hand was cold in hers, but when he gave her fingers an answering squeeze, Nolie felt a little warmer. And maybe he did, too, because after a moment, he smiled. "There are more video games than *Dance Your Pants Off?*" he asked, and smiling, Nolie pulled him toward the boat.

When they got back on board, her dad was looking at Albert really closely, and Nolie tried to give him a look of *Please do not be weird or a dad or a Weird Dad.*

And in the end, Dad just shrugged, going to stand next to Dave. Across the water, the *Bonny Bel*'s engines fired up, and slowly, the two boats chugged away from the island.

The fog was still thick around them, and Nolie clutched the rail, feeling like she didn't even want to breathe until the way was clear. Next to her, Albert was motionless, too, his brother's hat clutched in one hand.

The boats moved noisily over the water, engines rumbling, the smell of gasoline mixing with the salt of the sea, and Nolie thought she would probably always associate that smell with this moment, heading for the thick wall of gray all around them.

Or she would, if they ever got out of this fog.

And then, as both the *Caillte Cruise* and the *Bonny Bel* picked up some speed, the fog seemed to part like a curtain, revealing the deep slate sea and the soft purple sky.

Nolie let out a long breath, and next to her, Albert made a surprised noise in his throat.

Or maybe that was more Gaelic—it was hard to tell.

Turning to look over her shoulder, Nolie saw Bel standing at the stern of the *Bonny Bel*, her eyes fixed on the island they were leaving, and Nolie twisted to do the same.

The fog was closing behind them quickly, but just before it did, Nolie caught once last glimpse of the light burning at the top of the lighthouse.

And then the fog drifted, hiding all of it—the island, the lighthouse, the girl still drifting in its halls—from sight.

CHAPTER 32

"SO HOW WELL DO YOU THINK SIR WOOLINGTON IS GOING to adapt to America?" Bel asked as she put the stuffed sheep in question into Nolie's backpack.

"There's going to be an adjustment period, for sure," Nolie replied, "but I feel like his cute accent is going to take him far."

Bel smiled even as her throat hurt, looking at Nolie's bags packed and placed against the wall of her bedroom. Her flight wasn't until tomorrow, but it was, according to Nolie, "so early it's actually inhumane," so she was getting her things together this afternoon. Bel hadn't spent all that much time in Nolie's room, but it still looked so empty to her with all of Nolie's things packed away.

She thought that Journey's End was going to feel a little empty when Nolie was gone, too.

"You're going to email me every day, right?" Nolie asked, going to sit on the edge of her bed. She was wearing a long-sleeved green T-shirt with a red tartan heart on it, the green nearly the same color as the wellies she was wearing with her jeans. Nolie still had the purple wellies, of course, but about a week ago, she'd said she wanted one pair of "proper Scottish boots" before she left.

Sniffing, Bel zipped up the backpack. "'Course I am," she said. "Now that I know where to find the best Wi-Fi in all of northern Scotland."

Nolie grinned at that, then picked up her phone. "Speaking of," she said, turning it for Bel to see.

There were, according to the screen, twelve texts in Nolie's phone, and Bel had a good feeling who they were all from.

"Ready to go?" she asked, and Nolie nodded.

"Let me grab my coat."

Downstairs, Nolie's dad was sitting at the kitchen table. His laptop was open next to him, but he wasn't looking at it. Instead, his head was bent over a book, a steaming mug of tea at his elbow.

"Hi, Dad!" Nolie sang out, but when she saw what he was reading, she came to such a sudden stop that Bel nearly crashed into her.

"Dad," she said, and he looked up, his eyebrows raised over his glasses.

"What?" he asked, a little sheepish, and Nolie's face broke out in a big grin.

"You totally stole my book, you thief!" Nolie exclaimed,

coming around to sling an arm over her dad's shoulders and read the page in front of him. "Learning all about the myth of the Minch, huh?"

Nolie's dad looked up at Bel and winked. "Let's just say that after certain events, I'm maybe a little more curious about this stuff."

Smiling, Nolie straightened up and walked back to Bel. "Mmm-hmm," she said. "Gonna have your own show here by next summer, all decked out with night-vision cameras and EVP recorders, hunting down Nessie."

"Never," Nolie's dad joked, but Bel saw him dog-ear his page before he asked, "You girls headed out? Need a ride anywhere?"

Nolie shook her head, pulling on her jacket. "We're walking down to the village," she told her dad, and he nodded, glancing out the window. The day was bright and sunny, the hills surrounding the village emerald green, the sky a dazzling blue. "Be back by supper," he told Nolie. "I was thinking fish and chips for your last night here."

"And *I* am thinking that's a genius idea, Genius Dad," Nolie said, and her dad gave her a little salute before she pulled Bel toward the door.

Once they were outside, Bel shoved her hands in her pockets and glanced over at Nolie. "Things seem good there," she ventured, and Nolie shrugged.

"They were never *bad*, I guess," she said, "but yeah,

apparently saving Dad from a magical fog island has been good for our general father-daughter bonding."

That made Bel laugh, and the two of them headed down the hill to the city center. The Boundary was still there, hugging close to its rocky island, and Bel kept an eye on it as they walked. The *Bonny Bel* was out there, too, white against the dark water and blue sky, and even though no one on board could see them, Bel waved.

Things had been good at home for her, too. The story of the boats disappearing into the fog had created enough of a stir that tourism had never been bigger in Journey's End. Bel's mum said she thought it would all die down by the fall—especially since the town was purposely keeping the story kind of murky—but ever since July, things had been busier than ever, the *Bonny Bel* adding two extra trips to its usual rotation just to keep up with demand.

And it was positively *mad* once they were in the village proper. Cars everywhere, people walking around carrying the bright yellow plastic bags from the McKissick family's shop everywhere she looked.

"Oh, wow," Nolie said, nodding across the way at Gifts from the End of the World. "Check that out."

The line was out the door now. Earlier, it had been so crowded in the shop that Bel had nearly knocked over a rack of postcards.

"I know," she told Nolie. "It's been like that all weekend. Mum said we'd actually sold out of Sir Woolingtons."

"Oooh, so now he's a collector's item," Nolie joked, and then she stopped, lifting her chin a little. "Wait, do you need to go help her? Your mum, I mean. With the store that crowded—"

Bel cut her off with a shake of her head. "Nope. Mum gave me the day off, what with it being your last day and all."

"That was nice," Nolie said, "especially considering that I thought she was going to ground you for life."

Bel's mum had been frantic when the boats had come chugging back into the harbor after everything on the island. As soon as she hadn't been able to find Bel after the meeting, she'd had a feeling the two of them might have headed off to the Boundary themselves. Bel was pretty sure it was only the fact that everyone had come back all right, Jaime and Dad included, that saved her from being banned from ever getting *near* the beach again.

"She knew I wanted to get as much time with you as I could," Bel said. Then, afraid she'd get all choked up again, she tried to shake off any sad feelings.

"So what dance are we betting on?" she asked, dodging around a family all wearing those same Nessie hats she's gotten for Al. "The one with the arm thing?" Bel would've demonstrated if she weren't afraid she'd knock someone about the head. "Or the one with the jumping?"

"Hmmmm . . ." Nolie pretended to think it over, pressing one finger against her chin. "I think he's going to surprise us today," she finally said. "Break out something totally new."

"A special farewell-to-Nolie dance?" Bel asked, and Nolie laughed, breaking into a quick little dance of her own, jumping so that her feet crossed one way, then the other.

"Something like that, maybe?" Nolie suggested. "Really capture my spirit."

They were both laughing when they got to the arcade, and sure enough, there was Al, dancing his pants off.

He didn't have as much of a crowd this time, but then, over the past few weeks, Al dancing at the arcade had become a pretty common sight.

"He beat the high score again," Leslie said, coming up to stand next to them. She was holding a plastic bottle of soda, her long dark hair in a low ponytail.

Bel smiled at her, and Leslie smiled back, a little shyly. They still weren't back to what they had been before—maybe they never could be—but after the meeting and everything that had happened on the island, things had gotten better.

"After all," Bel had told Nolie just a few days ago, "if Cait can forgive the entire village for killing her, I think I can forgive Leslie for dumping me for Alice."

Alice was still around, just spending more time with Cara than Leslie now. Bel wasn't sure what things would be like once they were all back at school, but for now, it was good, and Bel was happy with that.

Not as happy as Al, though, grinning at the machine as he hit another step, his feet almost a blur on the pad.

The song ended, and Al raised his arms over his head in triumph. He was wearing jeans today, and a long-sleeved white T-shirt. His hair was a little longer, falling over his ears, and he just looked so . . . normal.

And cute, Bel had to admit.

He was going to be a regular fixture in the village now. He was living at Maggie's, the story being that he was her nephew from Inverness, come to stay with her. How long that would work, Bel wasn't sure, but for now, it was a good solution for Al, and he was definitely enjoying the twenty-first century. Maggie was teaching him how to use all those computers and tablets at her place, and just last week, she'd bought him an Xbox. It was a wonder he'd made any time for Bel or Nolie at all after that.

"I'm glad he's staying," Leslie confessed in a near whisper, and when she wandered off closer to the dance machine, Nolie slid in next to Bel and asked, "Are you ready for Al to be Journey's End's very own boy band?"

Bel nudged Nolie with her elbow. "I'm not the one with a crush on him," she said, and for once, Nolie seemed to have nothing to say, her mouth going slack, her cheeks flaming as red as her hair.

Giggling, Bel walked over to Al and draped her arms over the bar on the side of *Dance Your Pants Off USA.* "Bested a new routine, I see," she said, and Al looked down at her, pushing his sweaty hair back from his face.

"I don't think there are any more dances to do," he said, and then hopped down from the machine, his eyes scanning the crowd for Nolie. She was still hanging back, but when she saw him looking for her, she waved, and Al waved back, smiling, before his expression turned a little more serious.

"What is it you say when something isn't any good at all?" he asked, and Bel thought for a second.

"I'd say it was rubbish. Nolie would probably say it was a 'bummer.' What would *you* have said?"

"Would've said it was a nasty jar," Al said immediately, and Bel snorted.

"That's terrible," she said, and he gave a shrug, shoulders rolling underneath his T-shirt.

"Gets to the heart of it, though. Nolie leaving is a nasty jar."

"And rubbish," Bel agreed. "A nasty jar bummer of rubbish."

That made Al smile, and then Nolie was walking over to them. "What are y'all talking about?" she asked, and Bel answered, "Nasty jars."

Nolie pursed her lips, tilting her head to one side. "Do I even want to know?" she asked, and before either Bel or Al could answer, she jerked her thumb at the door. "Come on," she said. "If everyone is done dancing their pants off, I want to get some ice cream."

The lorry was where it always was, and all three of them got a soft-serve cone before heading back up the hill out of the village. They didn't talk as they walked, just enjoying each other's company, and Bel tried not to think about how tomorrow, it would just be her and Al.

Once they'd reached the cliffs over the town, the spot with the best view of the Boundary, Nolie sat cross-legged on the grass, and Bel followed suit. Al still stood, holding his cone with one hand, the other shading his eyes.

"This is going to sound stupid," Nolie said, "but it doesn't look scary now."

Bel watched the fog clinging to its island, rolling softly, but not spreading any further.

"No," she said. "It doesn't."

She thought of Cait, still in there, but knowing that the

town knew what it had done was wrong. Maybe feeling some kind of peace.

Leaning against Nolie, Bel said, "Do you think she's okay?"

"As okay as a ghost can be," Nolie said, and then Al came and sat on Nolie's other side.

"What are we going to do next summer," Al asked, "that can possibly live up to this one?"

Nolie and Bel both turned their heads to look at him. "Al," Nolie said. "Do not tempt me to spend all year researching some other kind of supernatural mess we can get involved in next summer. Because I will do it, my friend."

Al smiled, then crunched into his cone. "There's always Nessie," he said. "So we might see if my hat matches the real thing."

"Blue men of the Minch," Bel suggested, once again resting her head on Nolie's shoulder. "Or the Wulver."

"What's that?" Nolie asked, and Al answered, saying, "Oh, I know that one!"

"Werewolf," Bel clarified, looking back out at the sea. The sun was sparkling on the water, the sky still blue. "Leaves fish for people."

Nolie burst out laughing, nearly choking on the bite of ice cream cone she'd had in her mouth. "Okay, yes. Yes, I want to solve the mystery of the Fish-Leaving Werewolf.

I vote for that for our summer project next year."

"Or we could come visit you," Al said. "Sure there's plenty to do in America."

Nolie nodded, wiping her sticky hands on the grass. "Haunted houses of Georgia. Could work."

The three of them were quiet for a long time after that, staring out at the Boundary, all lost in their own thoughts. Tomorrow, Nolie would be gone, and life would go back to normal for Bel.

Well, not *really* normal. What they had done had changed Journey's End, but it had changed Bel, too. She had rescued her brother and dad, lit a magical lamp, and talked to a ghost. And maybe she'd always been comfortable being in the background of things, but that didn't mean she had to stay there.

Even if she didn't *really* want to go after a Wulver.

"I'm going to miss you," she said softly, and Nolie tilted her head back with an "Argghh."

"You're going to make me cry," Nolie told Bel, and sure enough, her eyes looked bright again.

Wordlessly, Bel hugged her friend, and after a minute, Al—Al, who had been weird about *talking* to girls when they first met him—wrapped his arms around Nolie, too.

"Hey," Nolie said from the middle of the hug. "This isn't really good-bye, you know. Once you've battled killer fog together, you're bonded for life. It's even better than summer camp for that."

And then she pulled back, looking first at Bel, then at Al. "So no matter what, we're a team now, right?" She laid one hand palm-up on her knee.

Al nodded, placing his hand on top of hers. "A team."

Bel looked at both of them, then back out at the Boundary again. For the rest of her life, whether it was here in Journey's End or somewhere else out in the world, she'd remember the three of them rowing out into that with nothing but faith and each other.

And she laid her own hand on top of Al's. "A team."

ACKNOWLEDGMENTS

THANKS AS ALWAYS TO MY WONDERFUL TEAM AT PENGUIN! Anna Jarzab, Katherine Perkins, Rachel Lodi, Elyse Marshall, and Tara Shanahan, I am so lucky to get to work with you, and I appreciate everything you do for me and my books.

Holly Root and Ari Lewin, thank you for believing I *could* write something without kissing or fire, and for encouraging me every step of the way. I am forever so grateful to have both of you in my corner!

Theresa Evangelista, your gorgeous cover showed me things I didn't even know I loved about this book, and that feels like its own kind of magic.

Thanks, too, to Victoria Schwab for going to Edinburgh with me, and for pointing out that a pub called At World's End seemed like a good sign that this wacky Scottish middle grade about a far-off spot might actually work.

Dave Edwards and Gwyneth Jones, thank you so much for being such wonderful hosts during our Hawkins Family Does Scotland Summer!

As always, thanks to my wonderful family, who have let me drag them to John o' Groats twice now in search of this book. I love you guys!

TURN THE PAGE FOR A SNEAK PEEK
AT RACHEL HAWKINS'
SPOOKY MYSTERY—

Copyright © 2017 by Rachel Hawkins

CHAPTER 1

OLIVIA

None of this was actually my fault.

I wouldn't have even been at Live Oak House this summer if it hadn't been for my sister, Emma. My *twin* sister, Emma.

Sometimes it's weird to look at someone who shares my face but couldn't be more different from me if she'd been born on another planet. Mom says that it's because we're twins that we're so different, that we're always trying to make it easier for people to tell us apart. I don't think that's true for me, but it definitely is for Em.

We're what's known as mirror twins. We're completely identical, but in reverse. The little brown freckle near my left temple? It's there on Em's face, too, but on the right. She's left-handed, I'm right-handed.

When we were little, our mom made sure we matched all the time—same little dresses, same hairstyles, all of that. It was only last year that Emma rebelled and started wearing what she wanted. I'd never minded matching, but if Emma didn't want to do it anymore, I told myself I needed to be okay with that. Then on that Saturday, the day that screwed everything up, Emma came out of her room dressed the same as me for the first time in ages. It was an accident.

I hadn't told Em what I was wearing that day, and she hadn't come into my room to see me before she got dressed. It happened that way sometimes, an easy thing to do since we still had a lot of the same clothes. We'd both worn jeans and the pale blue blouses Mom had bought us a few weeks before. I liked the blouse because of the little flowers embroidered around the neck, and Emma's favorite color was blue.

Honestly, I'd expected Emma to ask me to change, but that day, she'd just shrugged it off. "One more time won't hurt," she'd said, and I'd been happy about that.

Things had been . . . weird with me and Em for nearly a year by then. Not in a big way, really, but if I was pretty content being *EmmaandOlivia*, all one word like that, I could tell Emma wasn't. It had started in little ways—wanting her own room, her own clothes—but turned into wanting her own friends and her own interests, people and hobbies that it seemed like she picked because she *knew* I wouldn't like them.

Like Camp Kethaway.

Camp Kethaway had been Emma's obsession for months, ever since she'd seen a stack of brochures in the guidance counselor's office. It was your traditional summer camp—canoeing, arts and crafts, s'mores, all that, which had sounded like a nightmare to me.

Staying in the woods with a bunch of people you don't know? Forced camaraderie? No, thank you.

I'd told Emma right from the beginning to count me out of her Camp Kethaway plans, and I think part of me had assumed she'd scrap the idea. We were kind of a package deal, me and Em, so surely if *I* didn't want to do it, she wouldn't, either.

But no, Emma had just gone on planning for camp, begging Mom and Dad until they relented. She was scheduled to leave just a few days after the lipstick thing.

We were going shopping with Mom, something neither of us really liked all that much, except I got to spend time in the bookstore, and Mom let Em go to the Sephora even though we weren't allowed to wear makeup. Emma always said the trips to Sephora were "scouting missions," that she was learning what kind of makeup she liked so that when she *was* allowed to wear more than slightly tinted ChapStick—on our fourteenth birthday, according to Mom—she'd be prepared.

The lipstick she took wasn't even a color she liked. It was too bright, almost hot pink, and Emma didn't like pink. *I* did, though, and maybe that's why Mom believed me.

I can still remember standing there at the front of the store with Mom and Em, the security guard, and the cashier with the pretty blond hair, a bright streak of purple over one eye. Mom's arms were folded over her chest, and her face was pinched and tight, white lines edging her lips. Mom had never been this mad at us before, but then we'd never given her any reason to be before that day.

And really, I can't blame Em. Em didn't point a finger at me and say, "It wasn't me, it was Olivia." *I* was the one who said, "I did it. I took the lipstick."

Even now, I don't know exactly why I said that. Maybe it was because I'd known that Mom would punish Emma by canceling her summer camp. Maybe I thought Emma would think I was cool for owning up to a crime I didn't commit.

And maybe—just *maybe*—when I said I'd been the one to take the makeup, I thought Emma would fess up even though she had to know that would mean the end of Camp Kethaway.

Maybe I thought Em would pick me over camp.

But she just bit her lip while Mom looked back and forth between us.

"Livvy, this is just . . . It's so unlike you," Mom finally said, and I saw Emma flinch a little bit. I couldn't blame her. Was Mom saying shoplifting *was* like Emma? Sure, she'd been going through some changes lately, switching out new crowds of friends every few weeks, it seemed like, but she'd never really been in serious trouble before.

I just shrugged and said, "I wanted to be different."

I still don't know if Mom actually believed me, but she sighed and nodded, and that was that. Obviously no one wanted to press charges against a twelve-year-old, but that didn't mean I was getting off scot-free.

Camp Chrysalis had been a thing in Chester's Gap forever, and I remembered past summers, seeing kids in brightly colored T-shirts picking up trash at the park, cleaning up the area around the country club pool. Some years there were only four or five kids. Sometimes there were nearly twenty. The camp wasn't just for our town anymore, but had opened up to the nearby towns in the tri-county area as a "positive redirection" for kids who'd screwed up. It had never in a million years occurred to me that I'd end up there. I'd thought with Emma away at Camp Kethaway, I'd be spending my own summer reading, maybe going to the pool.

Camp Chrysalis met at the town rec center not too far from our neighborhood, and as Mom drove up that first morning, I sat in the passenger seat, fingers laced together, hands in my lap. A whole summer of picking up trash. Of people *seeing* me pick up trash. For something I didn't even do.

"Little different from yesterday, huh?" Mom asked lightly as we pulled into the circular drive in front of the center. I'd always hated this building, all squat and square and brick, with columns painted like crayons. Somehow all those bright colors against the dingy brick just made it worse.

"Definitely wish I were at Em's camp instead," I answered.

We'd dropped Emma off the day before, and when I'd seen the way she smiled at the little circle of cabins and the brightly colored banner flapping in the wind at the top of a flagpole in the middle of that circle, I'd felt . . . okay. It was nice that Emma was going to get to do this thing she really wanted to do. I could still have a good summer, even with Camp Chrysalis.

The feeling of okay popped like a soap bubble as we walked into the rec center.

Mom put her hand on my shoulder, squeezing a little. "It'll be fine," she said, and I nodded, my mouth dry.

Leaning down, Mom looked into my face, her brows drawn

together, and I saw it again, that same look she'd been giving me since the Lipstick Incident—like the truth of it was there if only she could see it. Mom knew me, after all. And she knew Em. And I think she knew who'd really taken that lipstick, but since I wasn't cracking, there was nothing she could do about it.

Finally, she sighed and straightened up.

"Okay, let's get you signed in."

The camp was meeting in the gym, and we walked down a carpeted hallway in that direction, stopping at the big double doors and glancing inside. Three kids were already there—Garrett McNamara, a blond boy a year ahead of me who I'd seen at school; a smaller kid named Wesley, who was in my grade; and then, coming through the doors on the other side of the gym, a very familiar face, and one I really, really didn't want to see.

Ruby Kaye.

CHAPTER 2

RUBY

Liv got sent to Camp Chrysalis because of something her sister did that she—totally stupidly, I should add—took the blame for.

Me?

I actually did the thing.

It's a long story, but it involved getting on the wrong bus on our school field trip to the art museum, then making a deal with this kid from a different school to switch pranks. You know, I'd do a prank at his school, he'd do one at mine, and we'd never get caught because no one is looking for a suspect outside the school, right? *Such* a good idea.

I'd gotten it from this old movie I'd watched with my grammy once. I used to go to her house after school every day until my mom was done with work, and one of mine and Grammy's favorite things to do was watch old movies together. Grammy wasn't very old, and most of the movies she liked had been made before she was born, but she was a sucker for anything black-and-white and spooky. In the movie, a guy gets on a train, and he and a stranger learn they each have a person in their life they wish they could murder. They decide to murder the other person's person, figuring that that way, no one can connect them to the crimes. Obviously, that was way more intense than what I wanted to do, but when I got on that wrong bus, I realized it was the perfect opportunity for something *like* that, at least.

I think Grammy would've laughed.

But the other kid, Harrison, was a total weenie and didn't do the prank at Yardley Middle School, while I *did* do the prank at Chester's Gap Junior High. While I didn't think it was *that* big of a deal (like, you can vacuum up glitter, even *that much* glitter, I'm pretty sure), the "vandalism" got me in serious trouble, and my punishment included Camp Chrysalis.

Honestly, I would rather have been suspended, and I didn't think it was fair that *my* school got to punish me for something that happened at *another* school, but then my mom said she'd add to my punishment if I kept complaining (no Xbox until my time with Camp Chrysalis was up), and no one needed that. So off to camp I went.

We met at the rec center gym on a really pretty June day, the kind of day when I should've been riding my bike or asking Mom to take me to the little park on the edge of town for a picnic and Frisbee.

Okay, so I'd never had a picnic or played Frisbee with my mom in my life, but that's not the point. The point is that there were a million things I could've been doing that were *not* going up to the rec center to do who knew what with Camp Chrysalis.

"They could be a cult, you know," I told Mom as we walked

through the blue double doors leading from the back parking lot. The air smelled like bleach and floor polish and that faintly sweaty smell that hangs around every gym, or at least all the ones I've been in. "We could end up doing some really weird stuff, Mom, and I might shave my head and change my name to Starflower. Do you want a daughter named Starflower?"

Mom sighed, and it was the bad kind, something I always thought of as an "H Sigh." It sounded kind of like "Heeeeeeeeehhhhhhh," and she used it only when she was annoyed with me.

Since around fourth grade, I'd gotten really familiar with the H Sigh.

"Maybe you should've thought of that before you were so destructive," Mom reminded me, and I frowned.

"Destructive? It was glitter! There's nothing destructive about *glitter*."

I might have gotten the H Sigh again then, but we were interrupted by Mrs. Freely. She worked for the Baptist church and had done a lot of substitute teaching when I was in elementary school. She also ran the camp, and while she was probably around my mom's age, I always thought she looked older. Maybe it was her hair, cut in one of those weird short styles that sticks up, but on purpose? Plus, it was an ash blond that made parts of it look gray. She was wearing elastic-waisted khaki capri pants and slip-on sneakers in the same hot pink as her T-shirt.

"Ruby, hiiiii!" she said, her smile nearly as big as the grinning smiley face printed on her tee. CAMP CHRYSALIS, the shirt blared. MAKING OUR LIVES BETTER ONE SMILE AT A TIME. Gross.

11

And then she handed me one of the shirts, and I started to think it was fine if I never played Xbox again so long as I didn't have to wear that creepy smiling head.

But Mom was looking at me, eyebrows raised, and I gave an H Sigh of my own, taking the shirt from Mrs. Freely. "Thank you," I said, and Mom lowered her eyebrows, relieved.

"We have got a busy day ahead, Miss Ruby!" Mrs. Freely said, and I remembered she was one of *those* grown-ups, the people who call kids "miss" and "mister," probably with a "buddy" thrown in every now and then.

She checked something off the clipboard she was holding, then moved on to her next victim, a kid I was pretty sure was named Wesley. He was in my grade, but the seventh grade had like five hundred kids in it, so it was hard to keep everyone straight.

"It's not going to be so bad," Mom said, leaning down a little closer to me. She smelled like green apple shampoo and the orange Tic Tacs she always had in her purse. "Hey, you might even make some friends."

"I have friends," I said, and Mom put an arm around me, giving me a little shake.

"Real friends, Rubes," she said. "People who can come over to the house."

Ugh. Like I needed a reminder that after Emma Willingham and I had stopped talking, my social life had been kind of limited. It's not that I didn't have friends—I totally did—just that I'd never really gotten all that close to anyone besides Emma. Between her and Grammy and, yes, the people I talked to online, I'd felt pretty complete on the friendship scale. But then Emma had gotten mad at me, Grammy had died, and all I was left with was DolphinWhisperer2005 and SailorMoonXX.

Stepping out of her embrace, I looked up at her. I wasn't going to have to do that for much longer—I was only a couple of inches shorter than Mom now, and since my dad had been tall, I had high hopes of towering over Mom by eighth grade.

"Internet friends *are* real friends," I replied, "and you do online dating."

This is a thing with me, that sometimes I say things before I've really *thought* about what will happen when I say them.

But Mom just laughed, shaking her head and pulling her purse up higher on her shoulder. "Okay, fair point," she said. "But I'm serious. You spend so much time yelling into that headset, and I'd like you to—"

"Yell at people in real life?" I offered.

Mom wrinkled her nose. "Not exactly. I just mean . . . Look, try to get some *good* out of this whole mess, okay? And Emma Willingham is here, see?" She nodded across the gym to the blond girl standing with her mom. "You and Emma used to be such good friends."

"That's not Emma," I said. "That's Olivia."

It was so obvious to me that I was surprised Mom had made the mistake. Emma wouldn't have been standing there with her head kind of down and her shoulders rolled forward, like she was trying to disappear into herself.

That was a total Olivia move.

I'd known the Willingham twins since I was really little, and used to be friends with both of them. Well, I always liked Emma more, but when we were younger, Olivia had been okay. It was only around fifth grade that she started to bug me, always seeming irritated when I was over at her house, glaring at me and Emma over the top of whatever book she was reading.

But then Emma and I had stopped hanging out last year, all because I said a certain boy who went to our school was cute.

Problem was, Emma liked that certain boy and apparently she thought me pointing out that he was cute meant that *I* liked him, which was *not true*. I was just . . . making an observation about the world around me.

So that had been the end of me and Emma hanging out, and now her sister was here, sentenced to the same summer punishment as me, which was maybe the weirdest thing ever. What on earth could Olivia Willingham have done to get sent to Camp Chrysalis? Forgotten to say please? Worn pink on Tuesdays instead of Wednesdays? Mom blinked at Olivia, clearly trying to figure out why the *good* twin was here. "Okay," she said slowly. "Then . . . maybe . . . you and Olivia could be friends again?"

I think that idea was even more horrifying than the pink T-shirt.

Read the whole seriously fun series from *New York Times* bestselling author Rachel Hawkins!

★ "As surprising as it is delicious."
—*BCCB*, starred review

"If Buffy the Vampire Slayer were Southern instead of SoCal, raised on good manners, Cotillion, and sweet tea—she would be Harper Price."
—*Justine*